Captain Picard pressed forward . . .

. . . as the shuttlecraft plunged deeper into the stand of old-growth crystals. Mammoth prisms rose like redwoods on every side of the tiny craft, and their aged facets tossed the light around like magical snowflakes. Picard peered into the sparkling gloom without success, until his eyes grew tired and began to blur. Then he saw it—like the red pit inside an apricot—a burning darkness at the crux of the mighty cluster.

As they drew closer, he could see that the Blood Prism had been broken, or it would have been much taller. Even this stump of a crystal was impressive, because of its deep scarlet hue. It was almost indistinguishable from the black crystal that clustered in the hollows to either side of their destination.

Pazlar had to slow the shuttlecraft down, because the procession had begun to bunch together. Picard heard a gasp, and he turned to the rear, worried that Troi was in distress. But the counselor was just waking up—it was Barclay who had his hand to his mouth, his eyes as wide as O-rings.

STAR TREK
THE NEXT GENERATION®
GEMWORLD

BOOK TWO OF TWO

JOHN VORNHOLT

POCKET BOOKS
New York   London   Toronto   Sydney   Singapore

This book is a work of fiction. Names, characters, places and incidents are products of the author's imagination or are used fictitiously. Any resemblance to actual events or locales or persons, living or dead, is entirely coincidental.

An *Original* Publication of POCKET BOOKS

POCKET BOOKS, a division of Simon & Schuster Inc. 1230 Avenue of the Americas, New York, NY 10020

This book is published by Pocket Books, a division of Simon & Schuster Inc., under exclusive license from Paramount Pictures.

ISBN: 0-671-04271-8

10   9   8   7   6   5   4   3   2   1

POCKET and colophon are registered trademarks of Simon & Schuster Inc.

Printed in the U.S.A.

For Coach John

Chapter One

LIEUTENANT MELORA PAZLAR HOVERED above a row of terminals in a weightless, cylindrical chamber inside the protective shell that encircled Gemworld. This chamber was a monitoring station which was usually populated by Elaysian and Alpusta engineers. The Elaysians were in residence, but now so was an away team from the Federation starship *Enterprise*. Melora hardly considered herself to be a member of *that* crew, having been on board only a few hours before her dreams had been invaded by the Lipuls' call for help.

Melora glanced at one of the screens. Far beneath the shell and its labyrinth of collectors, generators, pumps, and forcefields floated Gemworld itself—a dazzling, multihued cluster of spires, prisms, and archways. Seen from afar, her crystalline world was an awesome bauble glimmering in the vastness of space. From within, it was a forest of massive monoliths, dancing light beams, and perpetual shadow.

Not only was Melora's body suspended in midair, which was normal, but her mind felt as if it were suspended, too. She was reminded of the out-of-body experiences humans often claimed to have had, even though few of them ever took the time to understand such phenomena.

It wasn't surprising that the Lipuls' dreamships had first contacted humans, out of all the Federation species. Unlike Elaysians, humans were open-minded, even generous and outgoing. But like Elaysians, they could also be obstinate and blunt. That bluntness was now being amply demonstrated by the harsh words of Captain Jean-Luc Picard, as he lectured Tangre Bertoran and a handful of Elaysian engineers.

In standard Federation language, the captain had already told them they had the equivalent of eight days to live. Did her fellow Elaysians even know how short a time period that was? They didn't have *days* on Gemworld, in the accepted sense, only refracted sunlight and a strange sort of twilight in the shadows. Gemworld had been inhabited ever since the universe was young, and they thought they had surmounted every obstacle. How could her people possibly comprehend that their life expectancy had come down to eight rotations of a faraway alien planet?

She could tell by the concern on Reg Barclay's face that he understood their predicament—and the truth of Picard's dire prediction. Counselor Deanna Troi listened with her usual detachment as the captain finished his summation.

"That is quite impossible, Captain," said Tangre Bertoran, in a tone of voice usually reserved for small children who have told grandiose lies. The silver-haired Peer of the Jeptah shook his head in pity. "Thoron radiation is naturally occurring in our atmosphere. And in Earth's too, I understand. It couldn't harm all life on Gemworld, only those who spend too much time near the mutant crystal."

"Which continues to grow every day," insisted the captain. "Commander Data is not given to making errant predictions. Trust me when I say that we have to shut down the darkmatter collectors and the dimensional rift in eight days—by whatever means—or we'll all die. If we have to shut down the shell to accomplish that goal, then so be it."

Bertoran wrinkled his nose and forehead ridges as if sniffing a foul odor. "Captain, we don't talk about 'shutting down the shell,' even in jest. . . . That is like saying we need to destroy the Earth in order to stop a weed from growing. Yes, it will work—but at what cost?"

The captain gestured broadly, making it clear how frustrated he felt. "I don't want *anyone* to die, especially not two billion inhabitants. My first officer and chief engineer think that we can power your forcefields from the *Enterprise* for a brief period, taking over while the shell is turned off. You know how all those systems are intertwined—there's no other choice. If we're successful, Gemworld won't lose any of her atmosphere."

"And if you're wrong, we'll all be dead," replied Bertoran snidely.

"We have eight days to put something together," answered Picard, sounding as if that were plenty of time. "We have considerable experience with forcefields, and my people have already gotten a head start on this. Your people can help by making sealed shelters, bottling air—whatever is necessary. Believe me, I wouldn't suggest this course if I didn't think we could do it."

Tangre Bertoran grimaced his displeasure. "What you're asking goes against all my upbringing and common sense. It's akin to *murder.* I don't know, Captain . . . I need to see Commander Data's sensor readings before I agree to this."

"We've got them." Picard gestured, and Reg Barclay fumbled in a pouch on his belt, finally producing an isolinear chip. Melora smiled at the contrast between this gleaming storage device and the aged violet prism that hung from Reg's neck.

"Can you read isolinear chips?" asked the captain.

Bertoran sneered. "After we joined the Federation, it took us about two weeks to master your language and technology. Now you wish to destroy *ours* in a heartbeat."

"Your technology has turned against you," said Deanna Troi, speaking up for the first time since the meeting began. Hesitantly, the counselor floated down from the circular doorway, looking uneasy in her weightless state. "We wouldn't go to this much trouble to destroy you. The only thing that can destroy you is doing nothing."

Tangre Bertoran scowled and snatched the isolinear chip from Reg's hand. "Give me a moment."

He and his entourage retreated to a monitoring console, where they plugged in the chip and studied the data, muttering in low tones. Melora hovered overhead, uncertain whether she should join her fellow Elaysians or stay with her unfamiliar crew. Since coming back to Gemworld, she had felt increasingly torn between her duty to Starfleet and a natural inclination to protect her people and her homeworld. The two shouldn't be mutually exclusive, but Starfleet represented the whole Federation, not just one peculiar planet.

Her split allegiance had never been an issue before, because Gemworld had always seemed like a memory from a past life, something that would never intrude on her Starfleet commitments. But being here, visiting her old enclave, seeing the frightened faces and the crumbling, mutant crystal—it had become clear that Gemworld needed her more than Starfleet did.

For now, the dimensional rift not only threatened their solar system, but it could endanger the entire quadrant if left unchecked. Captain Picard had made it clear that he would sacrifice his ship and every soul on her planet to keep that from happening. And he probably wouldn't hesitate to use the *Enterprise*'s weapon systems.

Reg Barclay looked at Melora and smiled sweetly, jarring her out of her depressing reverie. His boyish, earnest face brought out a smile in her, and she realized how glad she was to see him again. Here she was—perhaps in the last days of her life—and she had met a perfectly charming man who doted on her and strove to protect her. In fact, he strove to protect *all* of her people, as proven by the shard around his neck.

He was an unlikely hero—and an even more unlikely acting senior engineer for the Elaysians—yet he performed both duties valiantly. Looking at Reg brought out a respect and affection in Melora that she had thought she could never feel for anyone. And her feelings were amplified by the guilt she felt over not being totally honest with him. . . . The last thing she wanted to do was to hurt Reg, or any member of the *Enterprise* crew. They were trying to help, but they didn't fully understand.

Did Reg know how she felt about him? Did it even matter—with all the obstacles they faced?

Yes, it matters, decided Melora. This should be a time to feel for one another—to seek love, and give it. What did it mean to fight for life if they couldn't enjoy the lives they had? She had always prized her lone-wolf status, but that was another change she was willing to make in her life. At least she could show Reg her gratitude. . . .

Melora heard whispers, and she turned to see Captain Picard and Counselor Troi deep in conversation, probably assessing the mental state of their hosts. One didn't need to be a Betazoid to know that her people were worried—even close to panic—as they confronted the worst threat their aged world had ever seen. Only an hour ago hundreds of Alpusta had died in a failed attempt to reverse the sabotage—but the shell had remained stuck in endless encrypted loops, its fractal programming and darkmatter collection gone berserk, feeding off the rift between two dimensions.

She tried to shake off the vivid sight of dead Alpusta clinging to the shell and floating in space, like pale seaweed in a tank of ink. The engineers had been too arrogant, too confident they could tame their environment yet again. Counselor Troi was right—their greatest creation, the shell, had been turned against them.

With a look of concern, Barclay reached up and squeezed her hand. "Are you okay?"

"I'm fine now," she whispered, squeezing back. Melora grabbed a handle on an overhead drawer and used it as leverage to pull Reg closer.

"What . . . what do you think they'll decide?" asked the Starfleet engineer, floating closely beside her in the upper regions of the cylindrical chamber.

"I have no idea," admitted Melora. In truth, she didn't think the Jeptah would allow the shell to be shut down, unless people were dying by the thousands.

"If they have an alternative, they'd better come up with it soon," said Reg urgently. "Although the last one didn't work too well." He cringed, as if instantly regretting those harsh words. "I'm sorry, I—"

"It's the truth," snapped Melora. "They've been arrogant, but now they're humbled. That's why I don't know what they'll decide to do."

Her gaze traveled to the clutch of yellow-robed Jeptah huddled around a monitoring console manned by Tangre Bertoran himself. From their hushed whispers and surreptitious glances at the away team, Melora inferred that the information gleaned from the *Enterprise*'s sensors was accurate and alarming. Had it been false, Bertoran would have already flung it in their faces. His hands were trembling as he pushed himself away from the console. His fellow Jeptah fluttered nervously around him.

The four visitors from the *Enterprise*—Picard, Troi, Barclay, and Pazlar—formed uneven ranks to meet the Peer of the Jeptah. Tangre Bertoran pushed off the wall and glided slowly toward them, his proud face looking craggy and hollow-eyed, as if he hadn't slept for a millennium.

"Your findings appear to be accurate," he said with grave understatement. "We weren't figuring the incremental increases and the full effect of the mutant crystal. When it breaks, even more thoron radiation is released. It would seem that our time is very short, although the effect of the radiation will vary from species to species."

"We still have enough time to close that rift," insisted Picard. "Let's assume that my people will be able to power your forcefields for the short time we need to reboot. . . . How do we turn off the shell?"

Bertoran heaved his bony shoulders and looked as if he had been asked to explain the theory of relativity to a toddler. "Although such a drastic measure has never been seriously considered, an ancient procedure was developed. It was assumed that this would herald the end of the world; therefore, the procedure to shut down the shell is rather arcane, going back to the Accords of the Ancients. That's when all six of our sentient species agreed to be equal partners in the operation of the shell . . . and the planet."

The elder Elaysian gripped the emerald-colored jewel floating about his neck, which marked him as proxy for the senior engineer of the Gendlii along with his other titles. He motioned with disdain at Reg and his violet gemstone. "The Holy Shards, crafted from the living crystal and encrypted with our first fractal code, are all that is required to deactivate the shell. But we need all *six* keys to plug into the Termination Link at once."

He sighed heavily. "We have two crystals in our possession—mine and yours, Mr. Barclay. The Lipul will no doubt surrender its key, but getting the others won't be so easy. Some of our neighbors can be difficult to deal with, and some of them are difficult to reach . . . especially now."

"And one of them is the saboteur," added Reg. "The one who started all this."

"It looks that way," Bertoran grudgingly conceded. "That makes our task all the more difficult."

"The Lipuls," said Picard, pointing to the Jeptah closest to a terminal. "Check and see if the Lipul engineer can meet with us."

The woman looked expectantly at Tangre Bertoran, and he nodded with a downcast expression. "Do the captain's bidding. Give them full cooperation."

Melora recalled their vivid encounter with the Lipul senior engineer. Was that only a day ago? A lifetime could have passed; she would never forget what the wizened being had told them: The shell is expendable, but not the planet. Take whatever course is necessary to close the rift.

Of course, the Lipuls could survive on Gemworld without any atmosphere, living as they did in the gelatinous marrow inside the largest prisms. The crew of the *Enterprise* would also survive. . . . They could hang around to vaporize billions of bodies and pick up the pieces of a dead world.

"My Peer! Captain!" called the Jeptah on the monitoring console. Everyone turned toward her or drifted in her direction, including the two dignitaries she had hailed. "I regret to say . . . that the senior engineer of the Lipuls has left the shell."

"When?" asked Bertoran.

"Eight shadow marks ago."

"That's a long time," muttered Picard, "even before the tragedy with the Alpusta. Why would the senior engineer leave now?"

"Why would it stay?" asked Bertoran with a shrug. "When there's danger, a Lipul always retreats to its crystal—that's the safest place."

Even that isn't safe, thought Melora, *and the Lipuls know it.* She vividly remembered the frightful dream that had brought the *Enterprise* and its well-meaning crew to Gemworld. She could still envision the Lipul in that dream, as it writhed in agony, choking in the polluted, inky marrow. She could see the crystal turning black—instantly, not one meter at a time.

"We'll simply have to find them all," declared Captain Picard, straightening his shoulders and his resolve. "That's four senior engineers we have to find and persuade to let us use their crystals. We'll need to visit the Lipuls, the Alpusta, the Yilterns, and the Frills."

"Plus one more," countered Tangre Bertoran. "Although I possess the shard of the Gendlii, I wouldn't feel comfortable using it in such a drastic manner . . . unless you obtained permission from its rightful owner."

Picard scowled. "You're the proxy—do we really have to do that?"

"In this instance, yes," answered Bertoran. "Let history show that this decision was not taken lightly and that the proper protocols were followed. Don't worry, Captain, the Gendlii will be the easiest to find."

"Where should we go first?" asked Picard.

Bertoran folded his hands. "We are about to send the body of Zuka Juno to the Blood Prism, to be consumed by the Progeny. You may think it odd to perform an elaborate ritual in the middle of this crisis, but Zuka Juno was a renowned member of our race. When you discovered him dead, it was a profound shock for our people. We must honor him, no matter what the circumstances."

The Elaysian managed a tight smile. "Your shuttlecraft can follow in the procession. This may be the best opportunity you'll have to meet the Frills in a diplomatic setting, although I suggest you should be very cautious. Melora can tell you more about them."

She nodded curtly to the captain, trying not to show her concern about encountering the Frills, especially in a time of chaos. Chaos was their natural state, and they might forget the Accords.

"Did you ascertain the cause of Zuka Juno's death?" asked Picard.

"His death was natural," replied the Elaysian. "A rare viral infection coupled with a weakened immune system. It was his time. Perhaps he has gone to light the path for the rest of us. If you don't mind, Captain, I won't be going with you to the Blood Prism. I'd prefer to stay here and work with your engineers, the ones charged with running our forcefields from the *Enterprise*."

Picard nodded. "That would be Commander La Forge, whom you met. I also left Data on the ship to help out with this project . . . and any other problems that might arise."

Captain Picard tapped his combadge and spoke briefly to La Forge, setting up the first of what were sure to be numerous meetings.

"The procession to the Blood Prism is leaving soon," warned Bertoran. "Perhaps you had better return to your shuttlecraft."

"Very well. We'll be in contact." The captain motioned with his hand and led the away team toward the circular doorway. Tangre Bertoran pushed off from the wall and darted in front of Melora, blocking her exit.

"May I please speak to Lieutenant Pazlar for a moment?" he asked. "It's some family business—of interest only to Elaysians."

"I'll be along, sir," she assured the captain.

Captain Picard nodded brusquely, then he herded Reg and Counselor Troi out of the room. As soon as the hatch had shut behind them, Bertoran looked intently at the young Elaysian.

"We can't let them turn off the shell, can we, Daughter?"

Melora shook her head, guilt and fear rising like bile in her throat. "No, Father, we can't."

Ducking his head and watching his shins, Reg Barclay paced the cramped deck of the shuttlecraft. He didn't want to pace, but he had to do *something* while they waited for Melora to join them. Besides, he knew he should enjoy this small oasis of gravity while it lasted. At the copilot's station, Captain Picard ran through a checklist while Deanna Troi alternately gazed out the window and at Reg.

When Barclay passed by her, she purposely stuck out an elbow to block his way. "You know, Reg, you might as well sit down. Nothing's going to happen for a while."

"Oh really? On . . . on what do you base that?" he asked nervously.

"Because we have to wait for a funeral procession, I believe." Troi again peered out the window. "And I don't see a procession . . . or anyone else for that matter."

Reg chuckled. "Oh, I thought you were using your empathy."

"I haven't sensed emotions for days now," replied Troi, frowning with concern. "I'm alive, but I'm changed . . . somehow."

"I'm sorry," said Reg with sincerity.

She shrugged, as if it were unavoidable, and then turned to gaze out the window. He leaned over her shoulder to see what she was looking at. At such close quarters, Deanna's raven hair should have smelled like rainwater and wildflowers as he remembered it, but now it smelled oddly antiseptic and bleached. Maybe she had spent too much time in sickbay. Or was she really different?

Shaking off these troubling thoughts, Barclay peered out the window and studied the pitted surface of the shell, with its swooping bands of metal and huge kidney-shaped windows looking onto space. There was no sign of the milling throngs that had greeted them outside the Ninth Processing Gate a few short days ago. *Gemworld is like a dying patient who has taken a turn for the worse,* he decided, *and the family members have gone home to make their peace.*

His gaze traveled starboard, and his eyes widened when he saw a blond-haired vision in billowing white garments swooping toward them. Melora caught the rails under the shuttlecraft and spun around like a gymnast, tugging with her arms and shooting deftly toward the open hatch. The smile on her face vanished as soon as she felt the artificial gravity in the hatchway. It was like watching a butterfly turn into a caterpillar, as Melora sank weakly to her knees and hauled herself with difficulty into the cabin.

"Uh, sir . . . C-Captain Picard," said Reg hesitantly. "Is it possible for us to turn off the gravity? I believe I'm getting used to weightlessness—I almost like it now!"

"No, no, that's all right," insisted Melora. "I could put my anti-grav suit on . . . if we have enough time."

"Nonsense," answered Picard. "You're the pilot, and you should be comfortable. Plus there's something to be said for 'When in Rome, do as the Romans do.' All hands, find a seat and belt yourselves in. We're going to shut off the gravity." He swiveled around in his chair, while Reg scrambled for a seat beside Deanna.

"That was very gallant of you," whispered the Betazoid to Reg.

Barclay squirmed nervously. "Um, thank you." He looked up to see Melora smiling gratefully at him as she waited in the hatch. He mouthed the words to her, "You're welcome."

"Turning off gravity," said the captain. Reg felt his body becoming eerily light. The hair on the back of his neck began to float, and the lap restraint was now the only thing touching him. Melora swooped into the shuttlecraft like a gust of wind and planted herself in the pilot's seat, fastening her belt with a snap.

"All right," she said. "Preignition checklist?"

"Completed," said Picard. While the two of them conducted business, Reg let out a sigh and tried to relax in the uneasy weightlessness.

"So Reg, have you told her how you feel about her?" whispered Troi.

He stared at the counselor, feeling somewhat annoyed at her accurate guess. Then he caught the twinkle in the Betazoid's dark eyes, and his anger faded. Deanna Troi was a hopeless romantic like himself, and he couldn't deny her an answer.

"No," he whispered. "What good would it do? We're looking at the possible destruction of her planet and all her people. I can't bother her now with my personal problems."

"Most people don't view a budding romance as a 'problem,'" answered Troi.

Reg sighed. "It is for me. Right now, the important thing is that we save Gemworld. It's such a special place—we have to help them."

"We're doing all we can." Troi gave him a weary smile. "I was ill for a couple of days, so I'm trying to catch up. Whatever happened to me has something to do with that rift out there. I just wish I knew what."

Reg lowered his head. "You saw what happened to the *Summit* . . . when they tried to rescue us?"

"Yes," she answered with a grimace. "I felt every one of those deaths. But now I feel something else—worse—oh, I can't explain it. We have to accept the fact that we're all alone here, that we might have to make some difficult decisions. I'm surprised we haven't found any other way . . . except to turn off the shell."

"We've been frustrated everywhere we've turned!" said Reg with a scowl. "Whoever sabotaged the shell thought of *everything*; they anticipated everything we've tried to do. And they're still out there—still at large."

"I'm sure that's why the captain wanted me along," answered Troi gravely. "Perhaps we'll get lucky and my empathic senses will kick back in. I'm not sure how much I can help without them."

Reg nodded, unable to think of anything to say. He didn't think their mission would be as easy as the captain was pretending it would be. Yes, the *Enterprise* had gotten out of tight scrapes before, but the enemy was usually one they could fight. Here, the enemy was nebulous but deadly—darkmatter from another dimension. Its most frightful effect was the crumbling black crystal that was decimating Gemworld. But it was the invisible radiation that would kill them all in a few days.

Reg swallowed to clear his dry throat and twiddled his thumbs. He had successfully changed the subject away from Melora Pazlar and to the destruction of Gemworld, but the question remained: *How do I feel about her?*

Oddly, the worse the situation got, the more he felt as if he were falling in love. That was an awful trick for life to play on him, thought Reg angrily, as if he needed any more convincing that fate was against him. *How can I tell Melora that I love her? With all the trouble her homeworld is in, she doesn't want to be distracted by personal matters.*

"According to scanners, several life-forms are approaching," said Captain Picard suddenly, causing Reg to jump in his seat. The captain peered at his instruments, then at the blue sky beyond the window, as Barclay and Troi leaned forward expectantly.

"The procession," answered Melora. "It's a large one. I know Tangre Bertoran said we could be part of it, sir, but it might be better to trail behind at a respectful distance."

"Use your judgment," said the captain.

"Yes, sir." In the weightless cockpit, Melora's fingers flew swiftly over her instrument panel as if she were playing an instrument. Everyone else peered out the windows of the shuttlecraft, watching for the mysterious funeral procession.

Picard glanced at his screen, then pointed downward. "Port side, coming from the surface."

All four of them craned their necks and bobbed in their seats to get a glimpse of a long, wavering line of creatures ascending from the blue depths beneath them. The line wended its way upward like a trail of drunken geese, but the ease of their flight belied their considerable speed. It seemed only a few seconds before Reg noticed that the creatures were much larger than he had first guessed. And they had yellow tails.

Moments later, he revised that opinion when he realized that they weren't birds, or even birdlike. In fact, they were really *two* creatures—and one was pulling the other. What Reg had thought were yellow tails were really yellow robes, so he could guess that the beings in the rear were Jeptah, the elite of the Elaysians.

But what were those fantastic creatures pulling them? As they drew closer, he was shocked to see that they looked like giant moray eels. Each one was two or three meters long, and they had massive, reptilian jaws full of jagged teeth. They ranged in color from vibrant silver to a milky white that appeared transparent. Wings that looked like gossamer fins extended over a meter from their bodies in several directions, catching air currents and stroking gracefully through the air.

Something sparkled along their sinewy bodies, and Reg realized they were harnessed in jewel-encrusted bridles. Golden reins trailed behind them which the Jeptah clutched like royal potentates.

"Frills," said Deanna in a hoarse whisper. "There must be a hundred of them."

"Eighty-six," answered Picard, checking the readouts on his screen. "Aren't they magnificent?"

"They're carnivorous," added Troi.

"Don't worry," said Melora, "we won't get too close . . . until after they've eaten."

Reg frowned, wondering if that was a joke or not. Melora wasn't really the joking type, although she spent a lot of time around humans. With their serpentine snouts and jutting teeth, the Frills did look as if they could eat anything they wanted—including visiting Starfleet officers.

The bizarre procession made straight for the shell, passing close to the shuttlecraft. Reg almost suggested that they close the hatch, because the Frills flashed him unsettling glances. Their eyes were cold and fishlike. *Natural-born predators,* thought Reg with a gulp. He noticed that a dozen Frills at the rear had no Elaysian passengers; their reins trailed loosely behind them.

No one in the shuttlecraft said a word as the funeral procession soared past and circled to a stop in front of the Ninth Processing Gate. The Frills seemed to preen as they spread their delicate wings and curled their flat tails. Reg still found it hard to watch anything but their jaws and teeth. The Jeptah remained at stone-faced attention, gripping their reins.

In due time, the large hatch on the gate opened, and a crowd of Elaysians fluttered out. They parted to allow a cadre of Jeptah to emerge, slowly pulling a man-sized pouch wrapped in crimson material.

"That is Zuka Juno," explained Melora. "They will secure him to the last Frill. . . . I've never seen a procession this large before."

"He was an important man," said Barclay.

"And now you have his job," added Melora.

Reg gulped, wondering if eighty-six Frills would carry him to his final resting place. With all the Elaysians in the crowd, only the Jeptah dared to approach the ferocious-looking creatures. As Melora had predicted, they tied the crimson pouch to the last Frill, which had had no rider before then.

The crowd around the gate parted again, and two Alpusta bounded out, still attached to the shell by their collapsible webs. Each one of them pulled several colorful bundles, which looked flat and circular, like gift-wrapped tires.

"Hmmm," said Melora thoughtfully, "it looks like they've recovered some of the Alpusta bodies. Today there are many dead to take to the Blood Prism."

The Alpusta corpses were secured to the remaining riderless Frills, each one taking three or four of the colorful bundles. In death, thought Reg, the large, spindly Alpusta were small and compact. Nevertheless, it took some time for all of this loading and tying, and several of the Frills began to writhe anxiously. Their Jeptah handlers spoke to them, and this seemed to calm all but a few.

Still, Reg felt considerable relief when the massive procession finally began to move again. Using hover-platforms to gain momentum, a cadre of Jeptah led the way toward the planet. As they gained speed, the Frills unfurled their silvery wings, caught the convection currents, and spread out in a curving line soaring downward.

"Prepare for launch," suggested Melora Pazlar.

Reg gripped the arms of his chair, but he hardly felt any movement as the shuttlecraft pulled away from the aged machine that encircled the planet. His stomach still churned, but he knew it was more from worry than from motion. Eight days was hardly enough time to explore Gemworld, let alone convince the entire populace to risk everything on a theory from a bunch of outsiders.

What if we fail? What if we can't communicate with the Frills or the other species? We'll have to turn our backs on two billion souls. Only a few hundred could be saved! That thought was enough to make anyone's stomach queasy.

As Reg watched Melora calmly piloting the shuttle-craft, he tugged helplessly on the crystal shard that floated from his neck. She was counting on them for so much—counting on *him* personally—and he was deathly afraid he would disappoint her. Barclay closed his eyes, hoping the nausea and self-doubt would quickly pass.

Stretching across the sky was a remarkable procession of giant eel-like creatures, towing passengers and gaily wrapped corpses. The boxy shuttlecraft fell into line at the rear, keeping its distance as the procession snaked downward toward the massive prisms and ancient clusters of Gemworld.

Chapter Two

GEORDI LA FORGE FIDGETED while he stood at attention in transporter room 3, Data still uncannily calm at his side. The chief engineer wished he could be down in his own department, actually working on all aspects of the shell project, making sure their emergency repairs to the reactor would hold. When time was of the essence he hated having to indulge in diplomatic pursuits just to get things started; but this first meeting with Tangre Bertoran was important. They had to open up lines of communication and cooperation if they hoped to beat the deadline.

"What kind of guy is he?" asked Geordi in a whisper.

Data cocked his head. "Opinionated, recalcitrant, arrogant, brilliant, forceful, argumentative, at the moment fearful—"

"All right, all right," muttered La Forge. "I get the idea. How did you manage to work with him?"

Data frowned slightly. "I told him the truth, though he did not seem inclined to listen."

"Ah," said Geordi, crossing his hands in front of him. "Thanks."

"Beam locked on," reported the Bolian transporter operator. "We're ready to transport."

La Forge nodded and pulled a tricorder from his utility belt. "Energize."

The operator worked his console, and a stout canister containing an instrument array suddenly materialized on the transporter platform. La Forge and Data both opened their tricorders and stepped toward the beeping, blinking apparatus.

"Pattern buffer matches up," reported the Bolian. "It appears unaltered."

"It sure does," agreed Geordi happily. "I think we're back in the transporter business!"

"But only for extremely short distances within our own forcefield," Data reminded him. "Interference is still too unpredictable outside this range."

"You're right there," answered Geordi. "But we have to do something to make this operation efficient, if we're going to be swapping people and equipment back and forth. Okay everyone, activate your boots."

La Forge pressed a button on his utility belt and firmly planted his magnetic soles on the deck. It felt odd to be wearing space boots inside the ship, while dressed in a regular uniform and breathing regular air; but they wanted to make their guests comfortable. "Ensign, go ahead and cut the gravity."

"Yes, sir." The Bolian again plied his controls, and Geordi felt a weight lift from his shoulders, literally. The only discomfort was an airy feeling in his stomach and a brief of moment of disorientation.

"Locking on," said the Bolian. "Two to transport."

A moment later, two columns of sparkling light filled the transporter chamber from top to bottom. The columns slowly materialized into two Elaysians, dressed in flowing yellow robes and floating lazily over the platform.

Tangre Bertoran smiled appreciatively as he stretched his arms and legs. "Thank you, Commander La Forge. This welcome—and your efforts to make us comfortable—are most gratifying."

With difficulty, Geordi lifted one foot and stepped toward his guest. "Let's hope we make some quick progress. Do you have the schematics for your force-fields?"

"Right here," said Bertoran, holding up an isolinear chip. "Out of all the systems on the shell, the force-fields are the most self-contained—they have to function no matter what. I believe you can patch into the injection couplers on the interior forcefield generators."

"We'll see about that," said La Forge, taking the isolinear chip from the Jeptah.

"That is, if your power-transfer conduits can be properly modulated to match ours."

"Just leave that to us," said the human, as he stomped loudly to an auxiliary console and plugged in the isolinear chip. Slowly be began to scroll through display after display of intricate schematics. Even with his enhanced vision, there was a lot of data squeezed into each rendering.

The human gave a low whistle. "I've never seen containment-field adjustment coils of this design, although I think I studied the theory at the Academy. I'm not sure they will interface with our reactor-port toroids."

"Just leave that to us," replied Tangre Bertoran, with a confident smile. "That's why this is a partnership. You produce the power; we'll find a way to plug it in. Can we work in here without going to the bridge or engineering?"

"Yes, this is as comfortable as I can make it for both of us." Geordi gestured around the transporter room. "We can beam anything we want into this room, including more personnel."

"I'm content with yourself and Mr. Data for the time being," answered Bertoran. "By the way, this is my assistant, Ansala Karpolin. She will be taking notes, so that we don't forget anything important."

The female Jeptah bowed obsequiously and pulled a padd from her sleeve. With a stylus poised over the padd, she waited expectantly to take a note from her master.

Geordi smiled. "For that, I've got Data."

The android cocked his head. "Welcome to the *Enterprise*."

"I've been here before," said Tangre Bertoran with a sly smile. "And I hope this really *is* transporter room 3, not some subterfuge set up to fool us."

Geordi tensed up and cleared his throat, as his forced cheer disappeared. "Uh . . . you're referring to your last visit . . . here?" Data looked puzzledly at him.

"Yes," said Bertoran, looking disappointed. "Did you really think I wouldn't check the logs of the Sacred Protector?" The Elaysian bowed his head, as if controlling his anger. "I realize that you later sent up a probe, but the shoddy holodeck act and the fake torpedo were beneath you. I was so distracted by the gravity at the time that I couldn't think straight, or I would have known it was a ruse."

"We needed to get you out of range of our shields as soon as possible. We couldn't make repairs while that broken crystal was pelting us. You didn't leave us much choice."

The Jeptah waved away the explanation with disdain. "I know it was Captain Picard who ordered it, not you. A clever man, your captain. I'm even with him, so let's move on. But understand that I won't forget your role in that deception."

La Forge decided to ignore the obnoxious scolding and get the exchange back on track. "You should know that we still have no idea what the consequences would be of using our weapons on that thing. It's likely to make matters worse."

"I only know you refuse to use your weapons on the rift," said the Jeptah with a sneer, "although you would use them on *us* or on the Sacred Protector. Your captain is an intelligent and imperious man. I hopes he's right about his claims."

The Jeptah moved his arms forcefully in a breast-stroke motion and caught enough air in his billowing sleeves to move away from the transporter. While the Elaysians found purchase to pull themselves along, Data looked quizzically at La Forge.

"I'll tell you about it later," whispered the chief engineer. "By the way, you were right about him."

Tangre Bertoran cleared his throat majestically. "When you mentioned your shields, that got me thinking. Can you hope to keep them on while you power our forcefields?"

"That is an excellent question," answered Data. "By our most conventional estimate, we would require all the power normally diverted to shields if we hoped to succeed. Perhaps if we docked closely enough to the shell, we could be included in *your* forcefields, which would allow us to power down our shields."

"Exactly how much power will we need?" asked La Forge, peering at the data from the isolinear chip. "Are these joule readings in direct correlation to standard newtons?"

"All in good time, gentlemen," said Tangre Bertoran. "First let me learn more about your ship and her capabilities."

Captain Picard knew they had traveled a long time when he began to grow bored with the dazzling crystal formations and tremendous monoliths they were passing en route to the heart of Gemworld. Light began to dim in the perpetual shadow of these hulks, but that only made the show more stunning and colorful. The multihued prisms refracted the shifting twilight into a curtain of aurora borealis effects. It was like flying down the center of a rainbow.

He rubbed his eyes, his senses overloaded with these remarkable sights, and pressed his lips together in concern. Without transporters, most of their deadline would be taken up by journeys like this, traveling great distances through a treacherous crystal maze. They could only fly the shuttlecraft at a fraction of its cruising speed, due to frequents clouds and clumps of mutant crystal. Even without that, it would be slow going behind the funeral procession. He wondered how the Frills and Elaysians were holding up during this grueling flight.

The captain was very glad that Lieutenant Pazlar was at the controls. She piloted the craft as gracefully as she piloted her body when she flew unaided, with tightly controlled swoops to avoid outcroppings and sharp corners. Picard could barely see the tail end of the flyers and their morbid cargo far ahead of the shuttle, but Pazlar made him feel confident they were on course.

He glanced back at Troi and Barclay, noting that they both seemed to be asleep—Troi dreaming peacefully, Barclay in a fitful, squirming doze. Barclay had spent more time weightless than any of them but just couldn't seem to get the hang of it. Placing the two of them on the away team had made perfect sense when he'd left the *Enterprise,* thought Picard, but now he wished he had brought a security team with a few Klingons on it.

Since he had no Klingons at his disposal, he had to rely on his diplomatic resources. The refusal of one senior engineer to cooperate could doom the entire planet. How could he make each of them see that without sounding like an alarmist?

Studying his instruments, Picard tried not to look at his chronometer, but finally gave in. They had been flying for over ten hours straight in a cramped, weightless shuttlecraft.

"We're actually making good time," said Melora Pazlar. "Now I see why they brought so many Frills with them: in case some can't make it. The Jeptah can drop off too, and take them back with their hover-platforms."

"How long do you suppose the procession is?" asked Picard.

Pazlar shook her head and smiled. "I don't know, but I think the Frills in front may have gotten there already."

The captain chuckled; then he looked hopeful. "Are we that close?"

"I think it will be less than an hour," she answered. "My memory of these routes isn't great, and I flew here by myself—without the benefit of shuttlecraft or Frills."

"A death in your enclave?"

She shrugged and looked wistful. "It happens a lot when you have three hundred or so in your family."

"Of course," said Picard, bowing his head. "If you're tired and want me to take over—"

"Take over?" She looked horrified. "I'm fine, sir, really I am. This is fun, flying the shuttle. I wish we didn't have an edict against shuttlecraft, but in many respects we're technophobic. Unless the gadgetry is really old, we don't want it."

The captain studied his new shipmate for a moment, then smiled. "It's funny how we adapt to our technology. When I first met you, Lieutenant, I thought you were a prisoner of your technology. I couldn't understand why you put up with so much hardship to be in our environment. Then I looked around at our ship, and the shell that protects Gemworld, and I saw *all* of us struggling to be someplace we shouldn't be. It must be part of our nature—and it makes you a lot like us."

Pazlar smiled, her V-shaped forehead ridges framing her attractive face. "I have been running from something, though. . . . I was never sure what, until I got back here."

"What were you running from?"

"It's probably something Counselor Troi would be more interested in," she answered. "Let's just say . . . it's a sort of provincialism. I love these people, but they're so mired in their traditions and protocols—the status quo—that you can't fit anything new into their minds. I'm probably not making any sense, am I, Captain?"

"On the contrary, I understand your point quite well," he answered, thinking of his own provincial upbringing in the French countryside. "I grew up on a farm that was much like your enclave. Although we didn't consider everyone to be family, we had a great many local workers, and the entire region depended on the winery. It was like an extended family. I could have stayed there and had a very nice life. Hard work, yes, but also the fruit of the vine."

He lowered his head and smiled wistfully. "Instead I fled to Starfleet—just like you. I had a brother who could never understand why I left. I didn't think I could wake up and see the same landscape every morning, no matter how beautiful it was. I like being a farmer—I enjoy holding the results of my labor in my hands—but I don't want to do the same labor every day. One thing about Starfleet—serving on a starship is seldom boring."

"I wouldn't know," answered Pazlar. "I'm never on one long enough to find out."

"Why is that?"

Melora paused to make a course adjustment. "I finally decided not to put people out trying to accommodate me. Wherever you go in Starfleet, you're surrounded by space, so I started looking for oddball assignments in low gravity. They're out there, and I'm qualified for a lot of them. Getting away from gravity for long periods of time has made me feel better, and my attitude has improved."

She scowled. "Until recently. Maybe I've been moving around too much, getting too rootless . . . too lonely. I can see that now."

"Where do you see yourself going in Starfleet?"

"I've never thought that far ahead—it's mostly been a matter of survival. It's funny, but the Dominion War was the first inkling I had that I could excel in Starfleet. Now I'm a mission specialist, which can be almost anything. That's good for the moment—one shadow mark at a time."

"We would be happy to have you on board the *Enterprise,* if you feel like putting down roots for a while."

She glanced at him, taking her eyes off the console and window for the first time. "Are you serious, sir?"

"I'm always serious about personnel matters."

Melora took a loud breath, and her forehead ridges deepened. "And I've been trying to figure out whether I should stay *here* and help rebuild my home. Assuming I still have a home—"

"You could have one with us," Picard said. He turned

back to his instruments. "But there's no need for a decision now—just think about it."

The captain heard whispering, and he turned around to see Troi and Barclay both moving at once. Their eyes were closed, and they pretended to be asleep; but their identical poses were highly suspicious. No doubt they wouldn't object to having Melora Pazlar on board full-time.

"There it is," said Lieutenant Pazlar, nodding toward the window, which was filled with a twinkling crimson twilight. "One of the oldest crystals on Gemworld—the Blood Prism."

Still floating in his seat, Captain Picard pressed forward as the shuttlecraft plunged deeper into the stand of old-growth crystals. Mammoth prisms rose like redwoods on every side of the tiny craft, and their aged facets tossed the light around like magical snowflakes. Picard peered into the sparkling gloom without success, until his eyes grew tired and began to blur. Then he saw it—like the red pit inside an apricot—a burning darkness at the crux of the mighty cluster.

As they drew closer, he could see that the Blood Prism had been broken, or it would have been much taller. Even this stump of a crystal was impressive, because of its deep scarlet hue. It was almost indistinguishable from the black crystal that clustered in the hollows to either side of their destination.

Pazlar had to slow the shuttlecraft down, because the procession had begun to bunch together. Picard heard a gasp, and he turned to the rear, worried that Troi was in distress. But the counselor was just waking up—it was

Barclay who had his hand to his mouth, his eyes as wide as O-rings.

He pointed a trembling finger out the port window at a weathered amber facet. "That . . . that wall . . . it's moving!"

"Let me see," responded Troi, who was in the best position to follow his gaze.

Picard loosened his seat strap and drifted upward. Once he stretched out, he could also see the rugged but glistening facet of amber. It indeed seemed to be writhing and surging as it tracked alongside the shuttle-craft; it looked like a wave teeming with fish.

"Just the Frills," said Pazlar. "It's possible they've never seen a craft like this before. They act like they're racing us."

"I'm sorry to get so upset," muttered Barclay.

"They *are* startling, the way they blend in," said Troi, rising to his defense. "They're almost transparent."

"These are young ones," said Melora. "The older they get, the more solid and dark their skin becomes."

"I'm curious," said Deanna. "When did you first know the Frills were sentient beings? I mean—that they were more than exotic animals?"

"They were here long before Elaysians," answered Pazlar. "It says something that they let us live while they destroyed many lesser species. Some scientists think that the Lipuls and the Frills are the only crea-tures on Gemworld that are truly native, tracing their lineage back to when it was an ocean world. They're not sure where the rest of us came from, although we were all here by the time the Ancients built the shell. Who knows? We might have come from drifting seeds or lost colonists. The Lipuls are the only ones who might know, but they've never kept histories in that fashion. It think it's all one time to them."

"So most of you are transplants," said Picard with interest, "albeit of very long standing. That explains the diversity." He twisted around and gazed back out the window at rippling wings moving across the face of a great, amber crystal. The Frills were alive, the crystal was alive, yet Gemworld was dying a death that had been put off for epochs.

Picard mused thoughtfully, "If Elaysians had developed on Earth, they might well have recognized our great apes, whales, and other creatures as sentient long before we did. That's a shortcoming of ours."

"It's true," muttered Barclay.

Like a jagged bullseye, the Blood Prism loomed before them, as they descended into the crux between four great spires. The weary procession hung limply in the warm air near the broken tip of the landmark, with throngs of swooping, silvery Frills darting among them excitedly.

Pazlar finally fired thrusters and stopped them about a hundred meters away. The swarming Frills circled the wrapped bodies like sharks, and a few dove at the bundles with open jaws; but they swerved away at the last second.

"This may seem a little barbaric," said Melora apologetically, "but the Frills have always been carrion eaters. This keeps them from starving. We have raised podlings for them to eat—it's sort of like a frog—but they haven't taken to the new diet. Their numbers have been shrinking gradually for a long time, and it's of some concern."

"If we don't fulfill our mission soon," remarked Picard, "there may be no shortage of carrion."

Pazlar bristled. "I got us here as quickly as I could, sir."

"I know," replied the captain, pushing himself back into his seat. "I'm not blaming you, Lieutenant, I'm just anxious to finish our business here so that we can move on. So let's make sure we talk to their senior engineer at the first opportunity."

"Yes, sir," Pazlar said as she gazed out the window. "It looks like the ceremony has started."

Picard turned his attention to the crowd milling in front of the Blood Prism. With the Jeptah floating and the exuberant Frills swooping about, the atmosphere seemed more like a circus than a funeral. Having conducted a great many funerals lately, Picard had to force himself to watch. No matter how many services he attended—no matter how noble the deceased—he could barely stomach them anymore.

It began with the Jeptah, who numbered about fifty, forming a circle atop the aptly named Blood Prism. Without gravity, they couldn't stand directly on the sheared surface, but they hovered as close as they could. The Jeptah monks began mouthing words and bowing in unison at appropriate times, although the shuttlecraft was too far away for the visitors to hear their words.

The bridled Frills—the ones who had brought the bodies such a great distance—remained quiet and unmoving. Their elongated bodies heaved and their jaws opened and shut enough to show they were breathing. *Probably still exhausted,* thought Picard. The other Frills glided away from the center of the proceedings, but they remained on the fringes, slithering back and forth with anticipation.

In unison, the Jeptah lifted their arms skyward, and Picard felt as if he could hear their anguished cry. A few of them waved, and the bridled Frills began to move—very slowly at first—dragging their colorful cargo down to the gathered Elaysians.

The circle of monks grew tighter as they reached up to accept the bodies; in doing so, they unharnessed the Frills and allowed them to fly away unencumbered. The scarlet bundle that contained the remains of Zuka Juno was the most sought-after prize—every Jeptah wanted to touch it. Flat packages containing Alpusta were also eagerly handled by as many Jeptah as possible. Using the golden reins and jewel-encrusted bridles, they tied the thirty or so corpses onto rungs carved into the crystal.

There have to be hundreds more Alpusta drifting in space, tethered to the shell by their own equipment, thought Picard. *Perhaps this small group of bodies is meant to stand symbolically for the others, the ones who couldn't be recovered.*

Suddenly one of the Jeptah drew a knife from the folds of his garment and slashed with abandon at an Alpusta bundle. A corpse spilled out, and one of the Frills from the procession edged over and took a hesitant bite. This strange ritual was performed a dozen more times, allowing the Frills who had carried the bodies to have the first taste. Even Zuka Juno's body bag was cut open and his body mutilated.

Despite the fact that they must be suffering from hunger and exhaustion, these invited Frills took only modest bites of the remains. They didn't seem to derive much pleasure from the ritual; in fact, they looked desultory. After they had nibbled their fill, the Frills wheeled about and let the Jeptah grab their sleek tails. They dragged the Elaysians to a ledge overlooking the sheared tip of the Blood Prism. It was more than a mere ledge, Picard quickly realized, because it had a mesh cage built into it.

The Jeptah filed inside the protective cage, and most of them turned their backs on the feast they had just prepared. An older, silver Frill suddenly spread all of its gossamer wings in a startling display of beauty, and it opened its mouth and squawked loudly. That was the first sound Picard had heard a Frill make in ten hours of traveling with them; he moved forward, unable to look away.

The mass of Frills who had been lurking on the sidelines darted forward. Ravenously, they attacked the colorful bundles and ripped them to shreds with their deadly fangs and jaws. Blood splattered against the dark-red crystal, adding to its dull luster. It looked like a feeding frenzy, thought Picard, but it was actually quite orderly. The Frills kept gliding as they fed, taking no more than their momentum allowed. Then they peeled off to make way for another wave of feeders. The area in front of them was so choked with teeming life that Picard could barely see the Blood Prism.

"At one time, the Progeny were a select few," said Melora with a soft sigh. "Now it's customary for the Progeny to eat very little of the meal, giving it all to the needy, which is everyone else. Even before the mutant crystal and the rift, the Frills were suffering."

"The Exalted Ones couldn't help them?" asked Barclay.

"They're a proud species," she answered. "As I understand it, they refused all offers of help . . . such as the podlings."

In a few seconds it was over, and all traces of the deceased were gone, including their colorful wrappings. A few Frills continued to dart close to the Blood Prism, but that was mainly for show or to pick off drops of blood floating in the air. Captain Picard hoped that the autopsy on Zuka Juno had been accurate, because there was no chance of doing it again now.

"I'd like to go on record," said Barclay, "that if I die here on Gemworld, I want a regular Starfleet funeral."

"Duly noted," said Picard with a grim smile. From the corner of his eye, he saw another procession—or at least another line of about twenty Frills snaking their way toward the Blood Prism. Then the feeders stopped their playful antics and again retreated into the shadows. Picard glanced toward the ledge where the Jeptah had taken refuge in their cage, but he couldn't spot a single Elaysian in the shimmering twilight. They seemed to have disappeared.

"Oh, no," said Melora, grimacing and turning away from the window. "I didn't know they were going to do a flesh-sharing."

"Flesh-sharing?" asked Reg. "W-What's that?"

Melora tightened her lap restraint and sank back into her seat. "A certain number of Frills are old and diseased," she explained, "or they've broken laws. Maybe they attacked another sentient creature. Whatever it is, they've been chosen for *this*." She waved her hand at the window, then looked down at her instruments.

"They're going to die?" asked Barclay in horror. "Be eaten alive?"

Picard didn't know how to answer, but he could tell by the look of disgust on Pazlar's face that Barclay had guessed right. The captain couldn't afford to look away, because he had to understand the Frills in order to deal with them. Self-sacrifice was obviously a strong part of their makeup, even if the form it took was repugnant. None of the condemned were fighting for their lives— they allowed themselves to be led like cattle to the slaughterhouse.

With alarm, the captain realized that the prisoner at the end of the line was floating erect and had legs. It was a humanoid, not a Frill!

"Is that an Elaysian?" asked Deanna Troi, giving voice to the question in Picard's mind.

"No," answered Melora as she studied her instruments. "I'm afraid my readings say that it's a human."

Chapter Three

REG BARCLAY WAVED HIS ARMS in alarm. "Are we going to sit here and watch a human be torn to pieces—eaten alive!?"

"No," answered Captain Picard, "not without asking a few questions. Pazlar, can I *talk* to the Frills?"

"Right now?" she asked in alarm. "I mean, yes, sir. They understand our speech quite well, but they have a hard time answering back. The best they can do is to beat their wings very rapidly to make vibrations that sound like words—it's very limited. But I don't suggest you go out there, sir."

"N-Neither do I," piped in Barclay.

"This shuttlecraft has a transporter," said Picard, nodding toward the stern. "I'll chance using it for a short jump. Don't transport me unless I order it or you see I'm hurt—I'll try to use the hatch. Take my place here, Mr. Barclay, and stand by."

"Yes, sir." Reg maneuvered out of his seat with some difficulty in the low gravity.

"Pazlar, take us closer."

"Sir, I advise strongly against this."

"Noted. Take us closer . . . slowly."

"Yes, sir." The Elaysian plied the controls, and the shuttlecraft edged forward into the crowd. At once, their actions captured the attention of the Frills; the closest ones fluttered away in alarm, only to circle back to check them out with cold, jaundiced eyes. The others also moved with increased agitation, and some of them began to track alongside the shuttlecraft as they had before, only now much closer.

Picard marveled at the sinewy power and grace of the Frills as they raced alongside the craft. They looked like pike he had caught in deep lakes as a boy—all jaws, teeth, and attitude. Only these creatures were five times larger than pike, especially with their wings extended, and they had the length and bulk of giant eels.

What am I going to say to them? Even the condemned Frills hadn't made any effort to get away, although they fluttered nervously at the end of their restraints. The human barely looked up at his would-be rescuers, preferring to stare at his feet as he floated helplessly in front of the blood-red prism.

"This is close enough," said Picard, judging that they were only about twenty meters away from the first of the condemned prisoners. Lecturing other life-forms was not his favorite pastime, but he hadn't come here to keep quiet. He knew he would never get a chance to address this many Frills again.

Once the shuttlecraft had stopped completely, he said, "Open the hatch. Then close it behind me. Stand by on that transporter for my signal."

"Yes, sir!" answered a nervous chorus consisting of Pazlar, Barclay, and Troi. The counselor had moved to the small, single-person transporter chamber in the stern and was checking its readouts. Her quick nod and encouraging smile told him that the machine would be working if his life depended on it.

"Go ahead," he told Pazlar. Without hesitation, she tapped the appropriate membranes on her board.

As soon as the hatch flew open, the closest Frills darted away in surprise. However, others came closer, and they moved past the open hatchway in waves, trying to get a look at the visitors and their vessel.

With his pulse racing uncomfortably, Picard grabbed the edges of the hatch and propelled himself into the open air. Fortunately, he had made so many weightless exits from the shuttlecraft lately that he was able to pull this one off rather gracefully. At least he didn't go tumbling head over heels, unable to right himself.

This action seemed to alarm the nearest Frills, who backed away as if certain he would use a weapon on them. He held up his hands and spoke loudly and clearly. "I am unarmed! I am Captain Jean-Luc Picard of the *Enterprise,* and I come here in peace, on a mission to save your planet."

He waited, but the only response came from a huge, silver-bellied Frill who cruised past him snapping his formidable jaws. The action was mimicked by several others, until the clacking jaws sounded almost like applause.

A cream-colored Frill rose up and beat its shock of multilayered wings very rapidly, like a hummingbird. A strange voice issued forth, sounding like a whisper coming from a wind tunnel. "Flesh comes to us," intoned the voice.

Picard heard some screeches, as the Frills called to one another. It could have been laughter, for all he knew. The condemned human was even watching him now, staring at Picard with hooded blue eyes that pierced through the gloom. Under the gaze of so many hungry eyes, the captain should have been unnerved—and he was—but he was also aware of an intense scrutiny that went beyond hunger. These beings were sizing him up for more than a light dinner.

"I must speak with your senior engineer!" declared the captain. "The one who attends to the Sacred Protector."

The creamy Frill beat its wings again, and the pseudovoice hissed, "After the feast."

Now the jaws started clacking in earnest, and several big Frills cruised dangerously close to him, their finlike wings brushing against him. Captain Picard held his position, realizing that any one of them could take off his head in a nanosecond and be on its way before his crew could react.

"I see you have one of my kind among you!" he proclaimed, motioning to the blue-eyed human, who dropped his head demurely. "May I ask what brought my fellow human to the Blood Prism?"

"Same as you," came a vibrating voice from above. "Seeking adventure . . . danger."

Picard tried to spot the Frill that had replied to him, but they kept swooshing back and forth like tigers pacing in their cages. He noted with alarm that a handful of Frills had surrounded the shuttlecraft, cutting off any normal retreat he might have had.

"If he has broken a law," declared Picard, "permit me to take him back to Starfleet . . . for trial and punishment."

"Nourishment!" replied a voice behind him. "No punishment!"

With increased agitation, the Frills began to sweep past him in teeming waves, flashing him more ivory teeth than seductive fins. Picard could feel his command of the situation slipping away—if he had ever had it—and he knew that some kind of dramatic gesture was required.

A sleek Frill tapped him with its tail as it swerved past, sending Picard into a backwards somersault. When he stopped spinning, he tapped his combadge. "Picard to shuttlecraft."

"We'll beam you out, sir!" came Barclay's frenzied voice.

"Belay that! Find a cluster of the mutant crystal and beam it right in front of the Blood Prism. I want them to crash right into it."

"Y-Yes, sir," answered Barclay. "There's plenty of it around. Locking on."

Picard tried to stay calm in the swirling, teeming mass of bodies and teeth. If the Frills weren't trying to eat him, they were trying to intimidate him—and doing an awfully good job of it.

When it appeared in their midst—a black cluster

shaped like a clutching hand—it shattered at the slightest impact and spewed foul, sooty residue into the air. That was enough to panic even these fearsome creatures, and the Frills scattered into the shadowy nooks and cruxes surrounding the Blood Prism. They abandoned the central space to a spreading cloud of noxious powder.

"There's your real enemy!" proclaimed the captain. "*That* is what's going to kill all of us—not hunger, not a ceremony. While we fret over the fate of these poor few, thoron radiation is building up in your atmosphere. In seven of our Earth days—not a long time—you will begin to die. Some of you may last a day or two, but for everyone it will be a slow, excruciating death."

Picard took a breath and noticed with satisfaction that the majority of Frills were squirming but listening attentively. He continued, "By now, you know that the programming of the Sacred Protector is stuck in a loop, collecting too much darkmatter and growing this mutant crystal. Your scientists have tried everything, but nothing has worked. We've got to shut off the shell for a brief period to reboot the system. It's our only chance."

He paused, expecting there to be disagreement and debate, but the response was muted—mostly the rustling of wings. The Frills weren't like the Elaysians, he decided; they were more accustomed to hardship and more accepting of it. Their penchant for sacrifice would serve them well in the days to come.

Without warning, one of the oldest silverbacks spread its wings and cut loose with a terrifying shriek. At once, it was joined by several others, screeching into the twilight. Instead of some massive primal scream, this seemed to be a signal to end the ceremony, for the majority of Frills turned and flew away, dissolving into the aged facets of the giant prisms.

Although he had hoped for an outcome like this, the captain was still amazed as he watched the fearsome beings disperse into the shadows. He didn't realize that a human was floating beside him, until he heard his snide voice:

"I guess you passed the test."

Picard looked curiously at the slight man beside him, noting that his blue eyes had been no mirage. He was handsome, small, and bearded—like a gnome or some bard from a bygone era.

"Weren't you tied up?" he asked.

"No," answered the man with a sly smile. "I was just doing a favor for the Frills. They weren't going to eat us—it was just a show for the tourists." He winked at Picard. "It makes the Elaysians more generous, if you know what I mean."

"You're not a prisoner?"

"No, they brought me along to see how *you* would react. You were being tested. Had you done nothing to help one of your own kind, or had you acted too rashly, they might have eaten *you*. These Frills are great kidders." The darkly bearded man grinned and held out his hand. "The name is Nordine. Keefe Nordine."

"Captain Jean-Luc Picard." The captain looked around nervously at his hosts, many of whom had not departed. "I would like to hear how you came to be here, but I have to see their senior engineer."

"Oh, he's probably being wined and dined with the

Elaysians," said Nordine. "In fact, that's where *we* should be. You'll get what you came for, I wager, if you have a little patience."

"What do you know about it?" asked Picard.

"Oh, we all know. It's a small planet, once you get to know it." The handsome man smiled obsequiously. "Say, I could sure stand to rest my feet on a spot of artificial gravity. You wouldn't have any on that shuttle-craft, would you?"

Captain Picard studied his new friend for the first time. Keefe Nordine was handsome and young, and he had a devil-may-care attitude that marked him as some kind of rogue. The fact that he would travel in Gemworld, and to the realm of the unpredictable Frills, branded him as a foolhardy adventurer.

"We have an Elaysian on board," he explained. "So we're not using the gravity."

Nordine shrugged good-naturedly. "Just as well, my muscles have atrophied anyway. I've been here so long, I probably couldn't walk if my life depended on it."

Picard frowned, looking down at the man's legs, which hung limply in the low gravity. "I can arrange to have our ship's doctor take a look at you. I don't know how much else we'll be able to do."

"You're too kind," said Nordine, bowing politely.

The captain lowered his voice. "Now how do I get them to take me to the senior engineer?"

"Just shout out your orders," answered the young man. "*Demand* to be take to him. The Frills respond well to bellicose braggarts. I should know."

When Picard hesitated, the man waved his arms in a

grand gesture. "Let me announce you. After all, you're an important man—you've got an entourage and two ships. Why should you do your own dirty work?"

Before Picard could protest, Nordine yelled, "Make way for Captain Picard of the *Enterprise!* All fear his wrath! Take him at once to the senior engineer. His time is *valuable!*"

"That's enough," muttered Picard. "I see a party coming toward us."

About a half-dozen Frills had left the ledge above the Blood Prism and were wending their way slowly toward the shuttlecraft. The captain tapped his combadge. "Picard to shuttlecraft. Come a few meters closer to me, so that I can get back in."

"Yes, sir," answered Pazlar. "Stand by."

Skillfully the Elaysian edged the craft in Picard's direction, opening the hatch as they came closer. Picard pulled himself to the hatch and stuck his head into the cabin. "Our improvisations have worked so far. I think we're going to see the engineer soon."

Melora lowered her head and looked chagrined. "I'm sorry, sir, I should have remembered that the Frills like to test their adversaries. I didn't realize it was a test."

Picard gave her a wry smile. "Don't let it bother you, Lieutenant. We muddled our way through. I can tell they're unpredictable."

"Who's your new friend?" asked Deanna Troi.

"A fellow traveler." The captain glanced at Keefe Nordine, who was keeping a respectful distance from the shuttlecraft. "When we have a chance, I want to take him to sickbay."

"More Frills are approaching," said Barclay worriedly.

Picard moved away from the shuttlecraft in time to see the first of the new procession of Frills come slithering past. Keefe Nordine moved his open hand from his nose outward in a kind of salute, and one of the creatures waved a wing in a similar motion. The captain made a mental note to remember that greeting.

Something glinted in the refracted sunlight, and Picard noticed that the last Frill in line—a silver brute with black-tipped wings—was wearing a blue gem around its neck. Tied with thick golden ribbons, the jewel bobbed enticingly as the big Frill flapped its shimmering wings.

Picard felt it might be a good idea to show his own colors, and he returned to the hatch of the shuttlecraft. "Mr. Barclay, come out here if you would."

"Uh . . . yes, sir," answered the lieutenant hesitantly. The gangly human stumbled out of the shuttlecraft into thin air.

Picard moved to reach for him, but he didn't really have a good place from which to push off. Keefe Nordine unfolded two pleated fans of Asian design, and pumped briefly with his arms until he reached Reg Barclay and steadied him.

"Thank you . . . v-very much," said Reg, straightening his uniform.

"Think nothing of it," answered the stranger. "The name is Keefe Nordine. Say, that's quite a bauble you've got around your neck. It's true then—a human has become senior engineer for the Elaysians?"

"That's what they tell me," muttered Reg. "It's only until we shut down the rift."

Captain Picard finally maneuvered to the shuttlecraft and pushed off, gliding toward Reg and catching him by the shoulder. "Hold it up," he insisted.

Reg did as he was ordered, self-consciously holding the violet shard at the end of its lanyard. As he watched this display, Nordine's eyes glittered just as brightly as the jewel.

The Frill senior engineer swerved close to them, and Picard gave him the salute he had seen Nordine give. The great creature twisted around and made an impressive return salute. Barclay hurried to repeat the gesture, getting it a bit wrong.

"Distinguished senior engineer," said the captain, "to save Gemworld, we need the crystal key you bear in order to shut down the shell. This is a very urgent matter—we wouldn't ask if it weren't necessary."

The silver-black Frill turned and spread its filmy appendages, drifting to a stop. With considerable effort, the sinewy creature beat its finlike wings, creating the hushed semblance of a voice: "We respect you. Elaysian proxy is our proxy. Take the key . . . and save us."

"He means you, bloke!" said Nordine, pushing Reg forward. "Take the gem."

With jerky, uncertain motions, Barclay untied the rope from around the Frill's neck. He didn't look pleased to be so close to those eel-like jaws and teeth, and his fingers didn't linger on the scaly skin. Still, he managed to take possession of the jewel in a reasonable amount of time, and he found a way to affix the rope to his other lanyard. Barclay was lucky the gravity was so low here, thought Picard, or the two hefty shards would be weighing him down.

We have three of them, counting Tangre Bertoran's. We're halfway home.

Picard considered asking the Frill engineer about the saboteur, the one who had started this nightmare. Of course, the primordial creature in front of him could well *be* the culprit, but there was no time for an investigation. They had cooperated by handing over the crystalline key, and that would be enough for now. The captain thought back to what the Lipul had said, when it predicted that the search for the saboteur would be overshadowed by their greater goal.

But the two were related. Warfare had taught Captain Picard not to underestimate the enemy—even when you couldn't see them. *Especially* when you couldn't see them. The motive was the hard thing to fathom, because it made no sense for any of the inhabitants of Gemworld to want to destroy the fragile planet.

Barclay was bowing and smiling at the flying eels, who swept around and past him in a slow dance of curiosity. He seemed to be enjoying the attention of these ferocious creatures.

"Mr. Nordine," he asked, "do you think it would be acceptable for us to leave?"

"Yes, I'd say so," answered the bearded man. "Am I going with you?"

Picard considered the matter for a moment. He knew nothing about this wayfaring stranger except that he was human and had been living on Gemworld long enough for his body to atrophy. By all rights, he shouldn't take a strange passenger on a difficult, dangerous mission, but he worried about how it would appear to the Frills if they left Keefe Nordine. They had gone to some trouble to present their lone human to him; perhaps they were subtly saying that it was time for Mr. Nordine to go home.

"Yes, you're going with us to sickbay," he answered. "Until then, you are to behave like a member of my crew. In other words, you'll obey my orders."

The bearded man smiled impishly. "I've never been much good at that, but maybe I can learn. Lead on, Captain."

"Mr. Barclay! Take my hand, and let's head back." Picard extended his hand to the lieutenant and pulled him into the hatch. Using his fans, Keefe Nordine made his own way into the shuttlecraft, and Pazlar closed the hatch after him. The Frills extended their circles, and were soon racing around the entire shuttlecraft as if trying to speed the visitors on their way.

"Hello," said Nordine, squeezing into the space between the pilot and copilot seats. "You're the most attractive Elaysian Starfleet officer I've ever seen. Pull away at a steady speed and give them a chance to race us."

Barclay was glaring at their passenger, and Pazlar was bristling at his informal tone. Still, she had the presence of mind to suppress her anger and look at the captain. "Sir?"

"He seems to know their ways," answered Picard. "Do as he suggests. Set course for the Gendlii enclave."

"That's some distance, Captain," said Nordine, "even in this boat."

"I estimate twelve hours or so," replied Melora with

a frown. "And that's if we don't have to take any detours."

"Captain," said Deanna Troi, "I'm going to stand in for Dr. Crusher and say that our pilot needs some rest before she undertakes another long flight. None of us could pilot this craft without rest."

"Very well," said Captain Picard, giving in to reason. "After we're out of Frill territory, we'll stop as soon as we can."

Keefe Nordine floated above the window and looked down at Melora Pazlar. "I know an excellent place to stop. Just cruise alongside the big amber crystal and take a right at its tip. That's about as far as the Frills will follow us."

Picard nodded to his pilot to go ahead, then he added, "Use all caution."

"Yes, sir. Everyone take a seat and use restraints." She looked pointedly at their passenger, and he saluted sharply and made his way to the stern.

Lieutenant Pazlar used considerable caution in guiding them up the face of the amber prism, thought Picard, as the Frills raced along beside them in a squirming mass. He glanced at Keefe Nordine, who was making polite chitchat with Troi and Barclay, and he wondered if *he* had used enough caution.

"So what are you doing here, Mr. Nordine?"

"Just what they told you," answered the slight man with a roguish smile. "I was seeking adventure and danger. Me and a couple of buddies came here—oh, it might've been a year ago, two years, who knows? We came here because we heard the Frills were the most dangerous game in the Federation."

"You're hunters?" asked Troi in alarm.

He smiled coyly. "Hunting is illegal in the Federation, you know that. On Earth, there are people who like to swim with the sharks . . . well, we wanted to fly with the Frills—test ourselves, be around danger. After all, Gemworld is about as far away as you can go and still be in the Federation."

"Where are your comrades now?" asked Picard.

Nordine frowned, and his youthful face looked a few years older. "The Frills tested us, just like they tested you. Unfortunately, I was the only one who passed. They ate the rest of them and let me live . . . as sort of a souvenir, I think. I probably would have gotten off Gemworld sooner, but the Dominion War started and the ships stopped coming around. We were sure we'd be invaded any day, but we were just ignored. Being here really felt like being at the end of the universe."

Barclay cleared his throat. "Um, what did you do to pass the test?"

"I was the only one who wasn't afraid to die," answered Nordine hoarsely. "For days, we caught no more than a glimpse of the Frills, then suddenly they came at us, hundreds of them! The others ran for it on their hover-platforms, and I was the only one who stood to face them."

He gave a hollow laugh. "My friends thought they could outrun them, but the Frills herded them into a dead-end crux. I could hear their screams . . . thank God I couldn't see them."

Nordine shook off the memory and mustered a charming smile. "They let me live among them and eat those awful podlings. Occasionally, they would even bring me meat, and I didn't inquire too closely as to what kind it was. I could've left, but none of the other enclaves wanted me. The Elaysians were very stand-offish. . . . Once the Frills figure you're worthy of being alive, they can be very loyal and protective."

A respectful silence followed this account, and Picard wondered how much of his sanity Keefe Nordine still had left. He seemed perfectly sane and understandably glad to be with his own kind again, but there was an unnatural brightness in his pale blue eyes. He could be a valuable asset or a considerable risk. Or he could be both. . . .

The captain's gaze traveled to his trusted counselor, and Deanna Troi looked back at him. She nodded almost imperceptibly at his unspoken order, as if to say she would keep an eye on their passenger and give him an evaluation as soon as possible.

"The Frills are dropping off," said Barclay, staring out the window.

Picard followed his gaze to see only a handful of younger, translucent Frills chasing beside them. By the time they reached the tip of the amber crystal—a spindly post with a new growth of mutant crystal—the last of the Frills had peeled off.

Melora brought them to a stop. "Now where to?"

"There's a fissure in that rose-hued crystal at two o'clock. It must have split open sometime in antiquity, and the marrow dried up. Anyway, it's a favorite place for people to camp before they encounter the Frills. Your back is protected, because there's only one way in. Still, it's best to keep a watch."

Picard checked the sensors for life-forms. "It seems to be clear. Take us in, Lieutenant."

"Yes, sir," answered the Elaysian.

The boxy shuttlecraft moved slowly between the tip of the amber monolith and another aged cluster of rose-hued crystals. A moment later, the tiny craft entered a fissure that was about thirty meters wide and half a kilometer long. As Nordine had predicted, the hideout was a rare sanctuary from the open spaces of Gemworld. The pinkish walls shimmered with refracted light, making it seem like some exotic spaceport.

The crevice contained a few remnants of past vagabonds, mostly rotten storage nets floating in the nooks and crannies like spiderwebs. Clumps of black crystal grew here and there, too. Without the marrow coursing through the great prism, it seemed dead and empty, like a dry cave on Earth. Melora guided the craft as deep into the fissure as she could, and she stopped it only a few meters from the narrow back wall.

The Elaysian opened the hatch and pushed herself away from the console, drifting toward the exit. "Since I'm the reason we're stopping, I'd better get started. I'll sleep outside, floating just under the shuttle. Then you can go ahead and turn on the gravity in here."

"Are you sure?" asked Barclay with concern.

"I'm positive," she assured him. "It will give me a chance to stretch out. With the struts, I won't even be visible."

"What about something to eat?" asked Reg. He fumbled in his utility belt for a package of emergency rations, which he dropped, letting it float from his hand.

Melora snatched the rations deftly from the air and gave him a grateful smile. "Good night." With a swift movement, she caught the edge of the hatch and propelled herself outward, climbing headfirst down the side of the shuttlecraft.

Nordine grinned at Barclay. "So, what's your secret? They make you a senior engineer and a proxy, and an Elaysian is *sweet* on you? You're really going over well here!"

Barclay turned redder than the rose-colored walls that surrounded them and stammered, "Th-that's no business of yours. I'm just t-trying to help them."

"Help yourself, lad, I always say." Keefe Nordine grinned insouciantly.

"His name is Lieutenant Reginald Barclay," snapped Picard. "When you address him, it should be as 'Lieutenant Barclay.' "

"Yes, sir." He gave them a mock salute. "Now, Captain Picard . . . you were going to turn on the gravity?"

"Yes. Let's all get situated in our seats."

As the others settled in, their passenger eagerly bounded into his seat and made sure his lap belt was secure. Nordine was beaming with such delight that he looked like a child at Christmas. "I'm ready!"

The others were safely seated, so Picard worked his board and restored artificial gravity. His body suddenly felt like putty oozing into a mold, and it took a moment for the captain's muscles and skeleton to respond and support his weight. He was surprised at how lazy and rusty those muscles had become in such a short time; every movement elicited a creaking protest of pain.

"Aaagh!" groaned Nordine, struggling to sit up. "I had no idea . . . I still weighed so much." With exuberance, he lurched unsteadily to his feet and promptly fell over, bouncing off Reg's chair and crashing to the deck.

Deanna and Reg moved swiftly to help him, but even their movements were awkward and uncertain in the newly restored gravity.

All three of them were panting with exhaustion by the time they got Keefe Nordine back into his seat. The young man, whose facade had been so brave and devil-may-care until now, had tears running down his cheeks. His lips trembled as he tried to speak:

"I waited so long for this . . . I can't tell you. But now I can't even *sit* properly!" He pounded with frustration on his useless legs.

"You'll have to be patient," said Deanna calmly. "That's why you need to see our medical staff."

"I'll sleep outside with the Elaysian," declared Nordine angrily. With a grimace of pain, he dropped to his knees, then his stomach, and dragged himself across the deck.

Picard refrained from helping him, afraid it would only make matters worse. "Try not to disturb Lieutenant Pazlar."

"I won't. I'll take first watch." The young man wiped a streak of tears from his cheek and with a great effort pulled himself out of the hatch into the freedom of weightlessness. He pushed off and drifted away to port, his body silhouetted against the shifting wall of pink crystal.

Deanna Troi sighed. "It's too bad nobody reached him sooner."

"He came here of his own free will," said Barclay uncharitably. The engineer stared out the window, his jaw working furiously. He was obviously jealous of Nordine being outside alone with Melora.

"One has to wonder," observed the captain, "whose punishment was the cruelest—his friends' or his."

No one had an answer to that. After a moment, Barclay gazed down at his feet and folded his hands, the frustration seeping from his angular body.

"Shall we get some sleep?" asked Troi, curling into a fetal position in her chair.

Reg Barclay stretched out in the aisle between the seats. "Oh, this gravity feels *wonderful*. When this is all over, I may take a vacation to someplace where the gravity is really strong, like Rigel VIII."

"Go to sleep, Reg," said Deanna with obvious fondness.

Captain Picard slouched into his chair in the cockpit and folded his arms, pretending to sleep but keeping one eye open. For a long time he kept that eye on Keefe Nordine, who floated about ten meters off port, his bright blue eyes watching the shuttlecraft.

Chapter Four

DESPITE THE RELIEF OF HAVING GRAVITY, Deanna Troi slept fitfully in the cabin of the shuttlecraft. As she twisted and squirmed in her seat, she wondered if her body hadn't already accommodated itself to weightlessness to some small degree—it seemed to resent the places where it had to rub against the furniture.

Deanna continued to worry about losing her empathetic skills, and she wondered if the loss was permanent. Even if they survived this crisis, would she be able to do her job effectively? Of course, most ship's counselors were not Betazoid—they couldn't sense emotions any better than anyone else—and they performed their jobs well. But she had come to depend so much on her inner feelings and instincts. Without the empathy to guide her, she would have to adjust her work methods. She would have to sharpen her interviewing and analytical skills to compensate.

Finally Troi fell asleep, lulled by Reg's gentle snoring. Her dreams started uneventfully, although they seemed to be in more vivid colors than usual. She dreamt of Will and her mother on Betazed having a luxurious dinner that had never taken place. After a while, these mundane scenes faded from her subconscious, and she began to dream of the soaring spires and fingerlike clusters of Gemworld.

She was a bit frightened, remembering that some dreams about Gemworld were very unpleasant, although she couldn't remember the specifics. Soon the gentle breeze bore her weightless body through the incredible passages between the sparkling monoliths, and all thoughts of danger faded away. Deanna was only mildly surprised when she passed through the protective shell and soared straight into space. In fact, she began to relax, because space was a familiar place.

Troi knew without looking that they were traveling with her. She looked around and saw the starscape fill with hundreds of ghostly shapes, billowing outward like the sails of a great fleet. The Lipuls were the shade of moonglow—with as little substance—yet they were *real!* Deanna knew that for a fact, although she couldn't lift her hand to touch one.

Where are we going? she wondered as they raced through the vastness of space. For the first time, Deanna realized that the Lipuls were not entirely self-sufficient—they needed structures built, computers programmed, their designs turned into reality. This unreal armada was in search of reality, thought Deanna; it felt as if she were reliving history.

Images, scenes, great trials and victories flashed before her gaping eyes, and she finally understood the long search. The eon of the dreamships had been a frightening time, but a wonderful time, full of travel, heroes, and adventure. However, distance was a great barrier, even for the dreamships, and there were so few inhabited worlds near them. Most of the creatures they found were low-level, not intelligent enough for contact.

Closer ... closer. ... The search centered on places close at hand but unseen. Without warning, Deanna felt herself moving with the Lipuls through a strange barrier, one she had never crossed before. Somehow it made her feel dirty, unwanted, as if she had swum a polluted river to come here.

But there were planets aplenty on the other side, all of them teeming with life in its fantastic variety. There was also a presence that was unseen but felt, and there were great swirls of darkness where even the dreamships could not penetrate. They grew confused and frightened, and they fled. She rushed off with them. Most, but not all, of the dreamships hurried to safe port within their ancient crystals.

Deanna recognized that terror. It had struck her only a few nights ago! With a gasp, she sat bolt upright in her seat and stared with bewilderment when she didn't recognize her surroundings. She tried to stand up, but her legs felt like she was moving through quicksand in slow motion, and she knew she couldn't escape.

"Counselor Troi!" said a stern voice, cutting through the fear and haze. "What's the matter?"

She concentrated on the voice, then the face, of Captain Picard. Only decorum kept her from falling gratefully into his arms. He put his fingers to his lips and pointed down at the deck, where Reg Barclay lay in blissful slumber.

Now reality came flooding back, even if reality was altogether strange at the moment. Deanna rubbed her eyes and slumped back into her seat. "I . . . I had another weird dream," she explained. "I can't help but feel it was sent to me by the Lipuls. It was like another history lesson."

"Is there anything I should know about?" asked the captain calmly.

"I don't know. . . ." She shook her head, trying to crystallize her thoughts. "Do you think it's possible for the Lipuls in their dreamships to cross into another dimension?"

The captain shrugged. "I suppose it's possible, but you're more of an expert than I am. Are you talking about the dimension on the other side of the rift?"

"I think so . . . maybe." Troi's eyes grew distant and troubled. "There's *something* over there—something scary. I think they were trying to tell me to stay away from it."

"But there's nothing that can help us immediately?"

Troi shook her head glumly. "No. Is there any way we can go see the Lipul engineer next?"

The captain sat back in his seat and folded his arms. "The Gendlii is the closest to us, and I thought it would be better time management to see the ones who might need extra persuasion first. I'm fairly certain the Lipul will cooperate."

"Of course," answered Troi, unable to refute the captain's logic. In truth, the most troubling part of her dream was the odd sensation that she had crossed over to that dimension before. It wasn't anything she recognized by sight; it was more like an emotion she had encountered before: mindless terror.

She had experienced terror before, like when the Borg were chasing her, but the source of that fear had been clear and present. The thing she was sensing now from that other dimension was a boogey-man-under-the-bed, thing-in-the-dark terror. She couldn't put a name to it, or a face, or a sound, because it gripped her beneath the level of conscious reasoning. Her primitive senses knew it was there, even if her regular senses were in a fog.

Ironically, thought Deanna, that was much like the ship's scanners being unable to pick up the dimensional rift near Gemworld. It was there, but its effects were felt below the surface, off the radar.

She felt strongly that they ought to go and see the Lipul engineer, but the captain's priorities were correct. Plus she had no idea if *that* Lipul was the one sending her these disturbing dreams, or if it was other members of that long-lived species. For the moment, she had no arguments to use with the captain, only nebulous dreams and vague fears. She felt as if she had a hole in her brain where some memory had been deleted.

Picard swiveled in his chair and tapped his instrument panel, which beeped and lit up at his touch. "I would like to let everyone keep sleeping, but we've been here over five hours. It's time to move on."

Deanna nodded and sat back in her seat, troubled at the way the dream was already fading from her conscious mind.

For most of that day's journey, Deanna had tried without much success to corner their passenger, Keefe Nordine, to learn more about his mental state. But he only wanted to talk to Reg Barclay or the captain, studiously avoiding both her and Melora Pazlar. Melora had her hands full piloting the shuttlecraft through the multicolored three-dimensional maze that was Gemworld while trying to avoid broken and mutant crystals. Deanna could understand that, but he had no reason to snub her.

Of course, he might have recognized her for what she was, a professional busybody eager to pick his psyche. It was hard to break in, since the others kept him talking. Curiously, the more she listened to his tales and personal history, the more she concluded that Nordine was a lazy young man with more time on his hands than sense. After several foolhardy adventures that he'd been lucky to survive, he had embarked on a doomed expedition. Now he was going home, traumatized, unable to walk. Nothing was said about his legs; it wasn't an issue, since they were again traveling without benefit of gravity.

At one point she caught a bit of Nordine's conversation with Barclay. They were whispering like a couple of schoolchildren in the back of the class, but her hearing was up to the task:

"I tell you, Reg, you don't know what you've got going here," insisted Nordine. "With those stones hanging around your neck, you are an important man. What were you before you came here?"

"Just . . . what I am," answered Reg. "A Starfleet engineer."

"One of the drones," said Nordine sympathetically. "I'll probably have to go back to that life now, but not *you*. You have conquered this place, Reg. You are like . . . the most important person on the planet! And the way the politics are set up here, incumbency is a solid advantage. On top of that, you're going to save the planet and be a hero. Man, you can have those jewels put in a crown."

"Do you . . . do you think so?" asked Reg, clearly flattered.

"Absolutely. You will have won your own planet— without firing a shot! Not only that, but you're the boss of the biggest bunch of snobs on Gemworld, the Elaysians, so even they're covered."

Keefe Nordine coaxed a piece of dirt from a fingernail. "Of course, you'll need a liaison, somebody who knows the territory. You'll need a larger staff, too, and some shuttlecraft to get around in."

"But I'm . . . I'm in Starfleet," said Reg with disappointment. "I *have* a job."

"Starfleet won't mind," scoffed Nordine. "They lose a midlevel engineer and get an alliance with the most important person on the planet—namely you." He winked at Reg. "Best way to keep your girlfriend happy, too. Good looks and power—that's a lethal combination."

"Good looks?" echoed Reg with an embarrassed smile.

"Just keep all this in mind," said Nordine. "We've got to save the planet first, right?"

"Right." Reg gave his new friend a nervous chuckle.

The ship's counselor smiled and closed her eyes, thinking that at least Keefe Nordine had the right priorities. If they didn't save the planet, his grandiose schemes of political patronage were all moot. Although she found Nordine's words repulsive, they fit the profile she was forming in her mind. He was a two-bit hustler and adventurer, ready to risk anything on a dare or for a quick killing.

She would advise Captain Picard to drop him off at the *Enterprise* and be rid of him . . . as soon as possible.

At the end of a long day, Melora still looked alert as she piloted the craft along the fractile lines of a curving, lime-green crystal. However, the rest of them were fading. Maybe it was the lack of gravity, or the lack of sleep, but something was making the passengers drowsy. Reg and Nordine had been sleeping for over an hour, floating in gangly heaps, and even Captain Picard struggled to keep from nodding off.

"Does it feel stuffy to anyone else in here?" he asked with a yawn.

"The temperature feels okay," answered Troi, "but I can't keep my eyes open."

"We're getting close to the Gendlii," said Melora, "and we've been using vented air from outside. It could be the spores."

"Spores?" asked Picard.

The Elaysian nodded and pointed out the window at the lime-green wall of crystal rushing by. "If you look closely, you can see some scattered bits of fungus, but the primal being is about five minutes from here. I'll cut off the vent."

Deanna peered curiously out the window at the luminescent crystal rushing past, and she did see patches of white marbled with black streaks. It looked almost like melting snow left at the side of the road.

"How can a fungus grow on the bare crystal like that?" asked Troi.

"Believe it or not, it can digest elements in the crystal and live off them," answered Melora. "The source being has rooted into the marrow of a giant cluster, and it's getting bigger and bigger. These little plants out here have no sentience—they come and go. There are some patches of a few hectares that can be said to have rudimentary sentience—like that of a bird—but nothing on the level of the source."

"How . . . how can you know if a plant is sentient?" asked Barclay.

Melora smiled. "You'll see."

Keefe Nordine bobbed weightlessly in his chair. Except for his flowing black beard, he looked like a little boy on holiday. "I'm glad to be along on this ride, because I never got over to see the Gendlii. The Frills didn't care for adventures like this."

"I hope it's not much of an adventure," muttered Picard.

"I wouldn't count on that," said Nordine cheerfully. "It's seldom dull on Gemworld."

They reached the end of the green prism and soared

into open space between the interconnected fingers and archways. "There it is!" called Melora. "Dead ahead."

It didn't even look like a crystal cluster. Instead, it looked like a bush covered with a heavy layer of snow, marbled with splatters of dirt. If that entire thing was the fungus, thought Troi, then it had to be a *million* hectares. It had to be the size of an island or a city. It was enormous!

"I've heard of giant fungi on Earth," said Picard with awe in his voice. "But they were ten hectares or so."

"Federation scientists think the spores could have been embedded in a meteorite or a comet," said Melora, "so the Gendlii came here on its own, an interstellar traveler."

"It sure made itself at home," said Nordine. "Wouldn't there be a lot of gravity around it?"

"No, it's a very porous, lightweight material." Melora smiled. "You'll see."

As the shuttlecraft drew closer, Troi marveled even more at the giant parasite, which seemed to have swallowed several massive prisms whole. It looked as if a thick sheet had been draped over the fingers of the cluster, leaving not a trace of the crystal underneath. It was a good thing the Gendlii was content to grow in this one area and not take over the whole planet, she thought.

The captain glanced at her with a puzzled expression, and she could almost read his mind: *How are we going to communicate with a giant fungus?* Not having an answer, she shrugged and gave him a helpless smile.

As they drew alongside the fibrous growth, it looked like the stalk of a mushroom as seen by an ant—

smooth and edible-looking, despite the occasional streaks of black. Pazlar didn't stop the shuttlecraft; instead, she cruised slowly along the bulbous face of the plant, as if looking for something.

"Are you looking for a place to stop?" asked Troi.

"No, I'm looking for the attendants. They must still be here." She smiled. "There they are."

They rounded a bulging corner and came upon what looked like a small enclave of Elaysians, with nets and ropes draped everywhere, holding meager belongings. Instead of roosting among the cruxes and nooks of the crystal, these Elaysians roosted among the pits and crannies of the fungus. At the approach of the shuttlecraft, about a half-dozen of them emerged from the shanties and drifted out to meet the craft.

"Don't be put off by their appearance," warned Melora. "They chose to live out here and devote their lives to the Gendlii. They're here to help people like us."

Melora popped the hatch and shot toward the exit before anyone could ask for an explanation. Picard pulled himself toward the hatch and exited after them, with Keefe Nordine close behind.

Deanna glanced at Reg, who toyed with his gemstones nervously. He didn't really want to leave the safe confines of the shuttlecraft, but Nordine had been right about one thing: Reg was the dignitary among them.

"They need you out there," she said with encouragement.

"I know," he muttered. "You go ahead ... please, Deanna."

"All right, but I'm sure there's nothing to be afraid

of." Pushing herself off her chair, the counselor floated slowly out the hatchway.

When she got outside and saw the Elaysian attendants, Deanna realized she had spoken too quickly. There *was* something to be afraid of. The poor attendants seemed to be blind, diseased, and horribly disfigured. Thick mushroom-like fungus sprouted from their eye sockets, ears, mouths, and every orifice on their bodies. Their simple robes could not begin to hide their deformed, emaciated bodies—the parasitic plant was growing all over them, eating them alive!

Still the Elaysians floated at attention, staring blindly past their visitors, oblivious to their awful condition.

Hearing a gasp behind her, Troi turned to see Barclay, gaping in alarm, his hand over his mouth. Troi rushed to his side and held his other hand for support, urging him to compose himself. Melora Pazlar looked at them apologetically, as if she hadn't expected a greeting quite like this.

When no one else spoke, Captain Picard cleared his voice and said, "I am Captain Jean-Luc Picard of the *U.S.S. Enterprise,* and with me are several crewmembers. One of them is Reginald Barclay, the acting senior engineer of the Elaysians and proxy for the senior engineer of the Frills."

At that declaration, one of the attendants lifted his disfigured head and listened more attentively. It was clear that he was blind and unable to speak, thought Deanna, and she wondered whether he could even hear them.

Picard went on, "We are here to inquire of the Gendlii—"

The attendant abruptly held up his hand, as if he didn't need to hear anything else. He waved to them to follow him, then he held out his hand and linked with another attendant. One by one, the somnambulant Elaysians linked hands until they could reach a slender green rope that was tethered to a distant corner of the enclave. They extended the rope to Picard, and he made sure that all of his crewmembers, including Nordine, could reach it.

Pulling themselves hand over hand, the six mute attendants and five startled visitors proceeded to traverse the length of the rope. In due time, they reached a portion of the fungus that appeared to be hacked up and stained with blood. *Can a fungus bleed?* wondered Deanna.

The chief attendant bent over the pit carved in the fungus and felt around with his hands for several seconds. He looked like a picky shopper at the grocery store inspecting the produce. Finally he broke off a chunk of unbloodied fungus and held it out to the visitors.

"Take it, Captain," said Melora to Picard.

He did as he was told, then he looked quizzically at the lieutenant.

"You're supposed to eat it," she explained. "That's how the fungus communicates to others."

Reg wrinkled his nose slightly, and Troi did her best not to reveal her emotions. "How do we communicate back?" she asked, unsure whether she wanted to know the answer.

"It eats from you," answered Melora. "You give it some of your blood."

That explained the blood stains, thought Troi, although it didn't make this procedure any more palatable.

Reg cleared his throat. "Will eating it turn us into, um ... like them?" He pointed to the disfigured Elaysians, whose faces and bodies had already been ravaged by the voracious fungus.

"I believe they get that way from ingesting the spores," replied Melora. "They've been living here for generations, trying to become one with the fungus."

"And doing a damn fine job," said Keefe Nordine. The young adventurer smiled impishly at Captain Picard. "If you won't eat that, I will. I believe this is a job for a crazy person."

With a scowl, the captain looked from Nordine's eager face to the chunk of fungus, which was slowly turning brown in his hand; it was hard to tell which disgusted him more.

"Anyone who eats *gagh* can eat that," said Troi encouragingly.

"Thank you, Counselor, for the vote of confidence." The captain popped the piece of fungus into his mouth and chewed with difficulty, as if it were quite dry and tasteless. With a look of resolve, he swallowed the mouthful of food.

Was it Deanna's imagination, or did a smile creep across the blighted face of the chief attendant?

Chapter Five

CAPTAIN PICARD SEEMED to be floating in a soundless chamber, surrounded by his comrades but unable to hear them. The only thing he heard was his own artificial heart, pumping in his ears. He tried to focus on the shuttlecraft, but it kept fading in and out of his vision, replaced by the sight of an aquamarine sea coursing with dozens of amorphous Lipuls. He didn't feel at all intoxicated, but rather as if another consciousness were intruding on his own. Picard knew he shouldn't resist it, but it was hard to let go . . . after his experience with the Borg.

When he began to feel sick to his stomach, he realized that he had to let go. He was a long way from sickbay. So the captain closed his eyes and attempted to clear his mind, trying not to be distracted by the concerned people around him.

"Welcome," said his own voice in his mind. "You have sought me for a reason, which I do not know. I know nothing about you. You have me at a disadvantage. Please let me taste you, then we will continue. If you have a question you wish to ask me, phrase it in your mind very clearly when you make the offering. I wish to meet everyone in your party, so ask them all to make an offering in turn. My attendants will help you. Blessings to you."

Like snapping out of a dream, Picard woke up and looked at his shipmates, who gaped at him with amazement and concern. "Are you all right, sir?" asked Deanna.

"Yes," he said, beating himself on the chest. He was especially glad to see that the nausea had passed. Briefly, he repeated what the voice in his head had told him.

"Are you . . . are you going to give it your blood?" asked Reg.

"Yes, I believe I will," answered Picard. "I want the Gendlii to know me. He asked that all of us do the same."

Barclay gulped. "Are you sure you didn't misunderstand him, sir?"

"No, I didn't. We all must think of a question, too. I'm going to think about the problem with the rift. I'll ask whether the Gendlii knows about it."

Before he could think too long or too clearly about what he was about to do, Picard reached for the hand of the chief attendant, who grasped his hand firmly in return. With a deft movement of his other hand, he slit the tip of Picard's thumb with an unseen blade and plunged his digit into the fungus.

Picard tried not to squirm, wondering how long it was going to take to feed the Gendlii his thoughts. The cut had felt painful at first, but now the pain had begun to subside. He wondered whether the Gendlii had some sort of natural anesthetic built into its chemistry.

Without fanfare, the attendant released his hand, and Picard pressed his thumb against his chest to stanch the blood. He smiled sheepishly at his shipmates. "Of course, that's why captains wear red tunics—so the crew won't see us bleed."

"It doesn't work very well," said Melora.

Another attendant bent down and pulled a chunk from the fungus, offering it to Picard. This piece was larger, about the size of a biscuit, and the captain needed three bites to eat it all. Oddly, it didn't taste as dry and bland as the first chunk had.

Time seemed to pass slowly, with everyone watching him, and the captain wondered whether he had gotten an ineffective piece of fungus. Perhaps he wasn't all that receptive to the voice of the Gendlii. Without warning, a bright light flashed behind his eyes, and he gasped. When his vision cleared, he was in a dark place, looking at a duplicate of himself; but his twin was dressed in a blazing white robe like some kind of god.

This radiant double beamed at him with delight. "Now I know you, Captain Jean-Luc Picard! I know all about you, and how you think. I know why you've come here . . . but why did you wait so long? Never mind. Our time is short, but you know that already. Although I never leave this place, I hear a great deal, and

I know our world has enemies. They have never shown themselves until now, but now they are determined to destroy us."

The apparition changed shapes and became a large Alpusta, bobbing on its multitude of spindly legs. "I will tell my proxy to cooperate with your mission. Inform my attendant that you must take an offering with you. It is for Tangre Bertoran. May the wind currents flow with you, Captain Jean-Luc Picard."

The human blinked his eyes, and he was awake, floating among his away team and the half-dozen attendants, whose faces were covered with the same substance he had just eaten. As ordered, he turned to the closest one and said, "I need an offering to take with me, for the proxy."

The disfigured Elaysian nodded and tapped a colleague, who reached into a pouch around his waist and produced a sophisticated specimen jar. Once again, the chief attendant felt the fungus with his hands for several seconds before finding just the right piece, which he broke off and enclosed in the jar. Finding Picard's hand, he relinquished the prized specimen.

"Thank you," acknowledged the captain. "Mr. Barclay, you should probably go next."

Reg gulped, but straightened his shoulders. "Yes, sir."

"It's relatively painless, Lieutenant. Just think of the question you're going to ask, and put out your hand."

Reg paled and held out his trembling hand. "I . . . I could ask it who sabotaged the shell?"

"Good idea." Picard took Barclay's hand and placed it in the hand of the chief attendant. He deftly drew blood—and a whimper—from the lieutenant before plunging his digit into the spongy fungus. When the attendant finally let him go, Barclay instantly stuck his thumb into his mouth and sucked furiously. Probably not the most sanitary thing to do, thought Picard, but instinctive.

After several seconds passed, another blind attendant searched for the proper chunk to feed Barclay. With reverence, he handed a muffin-size chunk to the engineer, who studied the offering as his complexion paled.

"Just eat it," urged Nordine cheerfully. "*You* can't do any wrong on Gemworld."

Barclay smiled bravely at Melora, who looked distracted by her own thoughts. With four or five hesitant bites and some slight gagging, he managed to get the fungus down his esophagus. Then he clamped his eyes shut, grimaced, and waited.

Despite having his eyes closed, Reg began to see things . . . ghostly bodies that coalesced into a procession of bishops and clergy moving through a grand cathedral, their robes trailing behind them. They were elegantly dressed, and were walking—which meant that this couldn't be Gemworld. No, this looked like a big holiday service in a place of worship on Earth, and Reg got a strong jolt of homesickness from the sight.

Then he realized that he couldn't be seeing this—it was only a vision. Nevertheless, it was perfect in every detail—the glimmering candles, vivid stained glass, well-dressed parishioners, and bells tolling while the choir lifted their voices. It was beautiful!

He started to cry, and a deep voice said, "Don't worry, my son, you are on the right path."

Reg looked up to see one of the grandest holy men from the procession looming in front of him, like an adult addressing a child. The white-haired eminence looked disturbingly like Zuka Juno, recently deceased. Self-consciously, Reg reached for the crystal the senior engineer had given him, and was relieved to find it still hanging from his neck.

"Didn't we teach that to forgive is divine?" asked the holy man in a kindly voice and crinkly smile. " 'Forgive us our trespasses, as we forgive those who trespass against us.' I am not asking *you* to forgive a trespass, as you are not the one who can forgive, but I am asking that you delay the search for justice until you have served the greater good."

Barclay gaped at the regal clergyman. "You *know* who tried to destroy the planet. They killed Zuka Juno, too!"

The apparition explained, "In this culture, I serve the same purpose as the priests of your culture. I am the Father Confessor for all of Gemworld, and I am told things in confidence. Or I learn things in passing. Sometimes I think I know too much, but, fortunately, I am large and dense, full of connective tissue."

The great man bowed. "Wear your honors well, my son."

A moment later, Barclay blinked awake and found himself surrounded by his comrades and a giant fungus that dwarfed the massive crystals. "Captain!" he shouted.

Reg almost blurted out what he had learned, then he

noticed Keefe Nordine, Melora, and all the Elaysian attendants, and he figured he had better be more circumspect.

Picard came forward at once. "Yes?"

The engineer bent close to whisper in the captain's ear. "The Gendlii . . . it *knows* who sabotaged the shell. And who killed Zuka Juno."

"Who?" breathed the captain.

"It wouldn't say."

Picard scowled. "Are you sure about Zuka Juno being murdered?"

"Well, no, not really," admitted Reg. "I don't think hallucinations are admissible in court. But it's a strong gut feeling . . . after that."

The captain nodded sagely and held up the specimen jar. "We got what we came for, the Gendlii's cooperation, so anything else we learn will be a bonus. That's the way I'm looking at it."

"Yes, sir," answered Reg, straightening to attention and suppressing his excitement. He wanted so badly to solve every puzzle surrounding this mission—making himself the hero—that he forgot about keeping focused on the goal. If in a few days everyone on Gemworld was dead, the identity of the culprit wouldn't matter to anyone except maybe a few obscure Starfleet historians. That's what the Gendlii had been trying to tell him.

"Can I go next, Captain?" asked Keefe Nordine.

Picard glanced at the two women, Troi and Pazlar, neither one of whom seemed to be in a big hurry to communicate with the Gendlii. He didn't entirely trust the young man, but the Gendlii had said that he wanted to communicate with everybody. The attendants waited patiently, staring straight ahead with eye sockets that had been devoured by fungus.

"Go ahead," answered Picard. "But I'd like a report."

Reg shivered, as he watched the dark-haired stranger get his thumb pricked and his blood fed to the plant. The engineer glanced at Melora, wondering why she was so reluctant to communicate with the Gendlii. Then he remembered what the creature had said about being Father Confessor to all of Gemworld, and he realized that contact with such an entity could be a humbling, sober experience. They hadn't known what to expect—but it could be that Melora had known all too well what to expect.

Does she feel guilty about something?

Before Reg could even try to imagine what Melora might feel guilty about, the attendants gave Keefe Nordine a piece of fungus to eat. A minute later, he entered an odd sort of trance, in which his eyes stared and his mouth moved but he was not communicating with anyone in his vicinity.

"This is almost like receiving long-range subspace messages from Starfleet," Barclay whispered to Captain Picard. "You can hear, and you can reply—but the exchange isn't face-to-face in real time."

"Just so," agreed the captain. He watched intently as Nordine finished his commune with the giant fungus, and the young man looked flushed with excitement.

"I can't believe I never came here before!" he muttered. "It might have kept me from going crazy."

"What did it tell you?" asked Picard.

Nordine gave him a troubled frown. "Some of it's personal, and I need to think about it. But it told me to help you if I want to redeem myself. And it told me to cut the cocky act—that it wouldn't impress you."

He laughed and shook his head. "This old plant is very wise. It saw right through me."

The captain turned to Melora Pazlar. "Would you like to go next, Lieutenant?"

"I've decided not to go," she answered brusquely. "Eating that stuff used to make me sick as a child. Besides, I have to pilot the shuttlecraft, and I don't want to be impaired."

"I don't feel impaired," answered Reg. "Not in the slightest."

"You don't have to get the shuttlecraft through all these prisms," snapped Melora.

"The Gendlii said all of us should go," Picard insisted.

"It always says that." She turned to the attendants and asked, "I'm not required to take the offering, am I?"

They shook their heads and intoned, "No."

The captain's jaw clenched with frustration, and he turned to Deanna Troi. "What about you, Counselor?"

"I wouldn't miss it." The Betazoid smiled gamely and offered her hand to the chief attendant. Reg looked away, unable to watch so much pricking and bleeding.

He looked back a few moments later, in time to see Deanna eating the fungus. Reg thought how selfless this was of the Gendlii, to offer bits of itself in order to communicate with all who came calling, seeking answers. How disconcerting it must have been for those first creatures who ate the fungus eons ago. They must have thought they were going mad, when all they were doing was meeting another living creature.

Troi's eyes rolled back in her head, and she seemed to be sleeping.

"You have been through so much," said a soothing, feminine voice—her own. "Just relax."

Deanna seemed to be floating on a raft in the middle of a gently rocking ocean, the same dark-blue sea she had seen in her previous dreams. It may have been billions of years since Gemworld had been a water world, but the racial memories of that time were surprisingly fresh.

"We have the same job, you know," said her own calm, understanding voice. "We minister to those who have been traumatized. You have been traumatized, Counselor Troi, and you don't even know it. To answer your question: yes, there is a hole in your mind. It's not an empty hole, it has been filled. If I could, I would destroy those brain cells so they would never bother you again, but I have learned never to expunge anything from my own memory, no matter how abhorrent and disturbing it is. . . . You may need it later."

She felt hands brushing her forehead and hair, and she opened her eyes to see Will Riker leaning over her. He gave her his warmest smile. Although entranced by the sight of him, she knew it wasn't really Will; nevertheless, his was the most comforting presence she could hope to see.

"Imzadi," said Will softly, "you are not alone. You have allies. I am one of them. Because you are like me, a sponge for the emotions and desires of others, your mind will always be receptive to unwelcome intrusions. When the time comes to face your fear, you must remember *yourself.* You must never lose track of your own identity, no matter how inviting it becomes to slip into the guise of another. The entity in your mind is powerful—but in the end, it is seeking what all the rest of us seek: forgiveness."

The water lapped over the side of the raft, splashing her and making her cold and uncomfortable. When Deanna opened her eyes, she was momentarily startled to find herself no longer floating on the ocean, although there was a creamy-white sea of fungus surrounding her.

"Are you all right?" asked Captain Picard.

"Yes." She nodded hesitantly.

"Did you learn anything we should be aware of?"

Troi's expression turned serious. "Only that . . . if I should ever lose my senses again, I'll need to come back here. Can you arrange for that, sir?"

"I promise," agreed the captain solemnly.

Will Riker didn't have the sensation of standing upside-down in his magnetic boots, but it was still disconcerting to stand on the exterior of the protective shell. From this vantage point, Gemworld looked like a bizarre hollow world—a swiss-cheese island made of metal, curving upward into the horizon. The pools of blackness were nothing but space, but they lent an eerie aspect to the sight. Above them was a pale blue sky and the distant outlines of the prisms, looking like a pile of pick-up sticks from a half-remembered childhood game.

Tangre Bertoran had adjusted his respective angle and was floating upside-down to talk normally to

Riker, Data, and La Forge. In the low gravity, he used one hand to open an enormous protective housing, revealing an array of electrical connectors attached to a pulsing transformer. "The injection couplers are the best place to patch directly into our forcefield generators."

La Forge nodded and consulted the padd in his hand. "We've already determined that we can modulate our power-transfer conduits to match yours. The containment fields are still a problem, though."

"What problem?" asked Bertoran. "This kluge will never meet all of your Starfleet specs, and it doesn't matter. If we don't do it, we die. If we fail, we die . . . or at least most of us. I suppose that you aboard the *Enterprise* will survive the loss of Gemworld's atmosphere, but the rest of us will not be here to cast blame because the containment fields were insufficient."

La Forge looked sheepishly at Riker and shrugged. "I suppose it's not critical. So . . . we should just plow ahead with our plans?"

"Perhaps we can arrange a test," suggested Bertoran. "You people are very good at simulations. Isn't there some way to test whether our procedure will work? I mean, within reason."

Riker glanced from La Forge to Data. "What do you think?"

"A test is feasible," answered Data. "We have already performed computer simulations. But unless the test is performed under realistic conditions, the data obtained will be unreliable."

"So," said Bertoran cheerfully, "we'll do our test under realistic conditions. Commander Riker, you should go ahead and dock the *Enterprise* as close as possible to the injection couplers, and we'll go ahead and expand our forcefield to include your ship. You won't need your shields anymore—that part we can verify."

The Elaysian continued, "Then we can do the hookups and even inject a token discharge from the *Enterprise* into the generators. They can handle it. After all, they're adjusting to the increase in darkmatter. The only things we won't do until it's time is shut down the shell and divert everything from the *Enterprise* into the forcefields. I assume you'll centralize your crew in order to cut down on life-support needs."

"That's right," agreed Riker. "We'll man the bridge and engineering, but most of the crew will be in the forward lounge."

Bertoran nodded sagely. "Then we will have done all we can. Should we plan for the test in forty-eight hours? That will leave us a few extra days, in case there's a problem."

Riker glanced at La Forge and Data, both of whom nodded their consent. then he surveyed the endless metallic horizon, unable to imagine the *Enterprise* being docked so close to the shell. But they had to start conserving power, and the shields were power-hungry. The *Enterprise* had undertaken more dangerous missions than this, and he could find no reason to object now, especially when it had been his idea. As Bertoran had pointed out, the risk was almost entirely to the populace of Gemworld, not his crew.

"Very well," he said. "Let's plan to test in forty-eight hours."

Tangre Bertoran smiled broadly and rubbed his hands together. "Excellent! I have no doubt, Commander Riker, that the *Enterprise* is going to save Gemworld."

"Where to next?" asked Melora Pazlar as she closed the hatch on the shuttlecraft. Of all of them, Melora seemed to be the most anxious to get away from the Gendlii, which Reg Barclay found rather strange. She had also been the only one in their group not to communicate with the giant fungus, even though she was the only native of Gemworld.

Granted that, given a choice, Reg wouldn't have indulged in the ritual tasting of each other's bodies either. But he was glad he had. Even though the Gendlii wouldn't reveal who had sabotaged Gemworld's shell, Barclay felt oddly reassured knowing that at least *somebody* knew. Perhaps when the crisis was over and the rift had been vanquished, they could spend more time with the Gendlii and convince it to tell them more.

"Lieutenant Pazlar," said Captain Picard, "what are the approximate travel times to Alpusta territory, the Yiltern enclave, and the home prism for the Lipul senior engineer?"

Melora checked her readouts. "Fourteen hours to the Alpusta. They're the farthest. About eight hours to the main Yiltern enclave, I'd say, and the home prism of the Lipul engineer is maybe ten hours from here."

"And the *Enterprise*?"

"That's the hardest to estimate, since it's not a common route from here. Let's say eight to ten hours."

Picard scowled, apparently not liking any of these

choices. Barclay knew it was because of the travel time involved. Time they couldn't afford to waste. Then again, they possessed the fastest means of transportation on this unique planet, so they had no reason to complain.

The captain's gaze traveled to Keefe Nordine, their mysterious passenger. He was sitting cross-legged, floating in the air like an Indian fakir and wearing a very contented smile. Of all of them, he seemed to have derived the most pleasure from his conversation with the Gendlii. Reg wondered what they had talked about.

"Lieutenant, take us back to the ship," the captain decided. "We may need to split up and take two shuttle-craft, in order to see all the engineers in time."

Splitting up sounded like a terrible idea to Reg, because he knew *he* would have to lead one of the away teams. After all, he was the acting senior engineer, the one with the crystal keys. The bashful engineer didn't really want to command an away team—or anyone else—but he knew he wouldn't have any choice.

Melora went through her preflight checklist. "Everyone, belt yourselves in. Prepare for launch."

"Don't you need to rest?" asked Deanna Troi.

"I'll rest when I get back to the ship," she answered. "I feel fine. The rest of you can sleep on the way."

"Am I going to see your ship's doctor?" asked Keefe Nordine.

"Yes, you are," answered the captain. "If she can't restore your atrophied limbs, then no one can."

Nordine grinned and pulled himself into a seat. "Then let's get this crate moving!"

Picard frowned and tightened his lap belt. "Launch when ready, Lieutenant."

"Yes, sir!" answered Pazlar, sounding eager to escape from the sentient fungus.

A moment later, the boxy shuttlecraft zoomed away from the cluster of crystals enshrouded in a bulging cloak of fungus. Reg saw Deanna Troi staring out a porthole window at the white apparition as it faded into the distance.

"What are you thinking?" he asked.

"I'm thinking that we have to save the Gendlii," she answered. "I mean, we have to save everyone on Gemworld, but there's something special about the Gendlii."

"I agree, I've never seen anything like it," answered Reg.

Deanna nodded absently and gazed out the window. "At least not in this dimension."

Chapter Six

AS THE SHUTTLECRAFT SOARED through the low gravity and crystalline structures of Gemworld, Reg Barclay noticed the captain studying the chunk of fungus in the specimen jar. Despite being in an airless container, it had already turned an ugly brown.

"I know some biologists and chemists on the ship who would love to analyze that," he said. "Do you suppose Tangre Bertoran would miss just a small piece of it?"

The captain smiled. "I think he would. We don't want him to get an incomplete message from the Gendlii."

Reg considered the idea of putting the offering through the replicator, which would give them a duplicate, but he decided not to suggest that. It would be too much like reading somebody's mail.

"Pazlar," said the captain, "what is our ETA?"

"Only about ten more minutes," she answered. "We're out of the densest part of the crystal, and I'm increasing speed. Captain, would you take over when it comes time to restore gravity and land in the shuttlebay? I'm not that tired, but I don't think I'm up to fighting gravity."

"Certainly," answered the captain. "You've done a marvelous job, Lieutenant. I would be glad to keep you on our crew, if only as a shuttlecraft pilot. We could make use of your other talents as well."

"Thank you, sir," acknowledged Pazlar. "But I still haven't decided what to do next."

Ten minutes later, the shuttlecraft swept into the spacious shuttlebay with Captain Picard at the helm. Reg looked at Melora and saw her wilt under the weight of the restored gravity. Her shoulders hunched, her head bowed, and her limbs seemed to contract—she shriveled before his eyes. He wanted to hug her and tell her it would be okay, but of course she had been through this transition many times before. Gravity didn't crush Melora's spirit, but it certainly impaired her body and changed her personality, not for the better.

What on Earth was he doing being in love with a woman who was so different from him? If they tried to stay together, where could they possibly live? Was there any chance of their having children? If Melora became a permanent member of the *Enterprise* crew, that would be wonderful for him, but what would it do for her? She might be able to adjust physically, but would she be happy?

Without warning, Melora looked up and gave him a radiant smile, as if she had read his thoughts. In that smile there was so much promise and tenderness that Reg felt certain that all obstacles could be conquered. They *would* save the planet—together—and then he would worry about his love life. To Reg, having a love life seemed more of a feat than saving a planet from a dimensional rift.

"Mr. Nordine," said Picard, "you stay here, and I'll send for a med team from sickbay to pick you up. Lieutenant Pazlar, do you have your anti-grav suit handy?"

"It's in the back," she answered. "Once you're all out, I'll change into it. If you don't mind, sir, I'd like to go to my quarters and get some sleep."

"Understood. Again, well done." The captain popped the hatch and bounded out, to be met in the shuttlebay by Commander Riker. Still looking preoccupied with her own thoughts, Troi followed after him.

"Hey, pilot, looks like we're two of a kind!" called Nordine to Melora. "A little gravity and we're grounded."

"Temporarily," answered Melora. She smiled at Reg. "You'd better stick with the captain."

"Yes . . . I guess so." Reg rose to his feet, feeling a bit shaky after so long in low gravity. He felt guilty leaving Melora behind, but he knew she was right—he had better stick close to the captain in case he was needed. Nevertheless, he took the liberty of stopping to squeeze her hand on the way out, and she squeezed back.

In the shuttlebay, Picard and Riker were hurriedly briefing each other in the kind of shorthand that old comrades often develop. Reg listened as they walked briskly toward the turbolift, and he was heartened to hear that the plan to power the shell's forcefields from the *Enterprise* was proceeding smoothly. They even had a test scheduled in thirty-eight hours.

"Is Tangre Bertoran currently on the ship?" asked Picard.

"Yes, he's in transporter room 3," answered Riker. "We've turned off the gravity in there to make it more comfortable for the Elaysians."

"Good. I have a message for him." Picard held up the specimen jar containing an unappetizing chunk of brown fungus.

"That's the message?" asked Riker doubtfully.

"From the Gendlii," answered Troi. "It's hard to explain unless you've experienced it. When this is all over, we'll have to go back there."

"Sounds good to me," answered Riker, giving Deanna a warm smile. "I haven't gotten to do any sightseeing. Maybe you'll show me around."

"Gladly."

Reg watched the interplay between Riker and Troi, fascinated. This was a couple who had certainly had their ups and downs over a long period of time, yet they were always able to work together with mutual respect and fondness. Now their romance was hot again; but even if it cooled off they would maintain their professionalism.

Picard, Riker, Troi, and Barclay entered the turbolift, and the captain directed the lift to transporter room 3. Then he tapped his combadge. "Picard to sickbay."

"Crusher here," came the response. "Welcome back. Were you successful?"

"Yes, as far as it went. Maybe we can grab some dinner in a few hours, and I'll fill you in. Right now, there's a civilian in the shuttlecraft we just landed, and he needs your help."

"Elaysian?" asked Crusher.

"No, human. It's a long story how he got here, but his limbs have atrophied from being too long on Gemworld. I said you'd help him."

"Of course, Captain. I won't let you forget that dinner invitation. Crusher out."

Another interesting couple, thought Reg. It was hard to tell how serious they were about each other now, but Picard and Crusher seemed destined to be together. Maybe it would take their double retirement from Starfleet to give them enough time to nurture their relationship. Looking at the trials and tribulations of these couples encouraged him, making him think that he could work out all the difficulties with Melora.

"Mr. Barclay, are you coming?" asked Riker.

Reg looked up from his thoughts and realized that the turbolift door had opened and everyone had exited except himself. "Yes, sir!" he called, rushing out.

A few moments later he was weightless again, and once again confronting the stern visage of Tangre Bertoran in transporter room 3. Maybe it was his V-shaped forehead ridges, thought Reg, but the Elaysian always looked as if he were frowning. Or maybe he didn't like being brought a day-old chunk of Gendlii to eat.

"This offering is for me?" asked Bertoran, studying the fungus in the specimen jar. "Very well."

Without much enthusiasm, he broke off bits of the fungus and chewed contemplatively until it was all gone. The Elaysian's eyes grew glassy for a moment, and he nodded several times to himself. La Forge and Riker watched with interest, having never seen this unusual form of communication before.

After a few moments, Bertoran blinked and was instantly alert. Without a word, he took the green shard from his neck and placed it around Barclay's neck. "Congratulations, now you're also proxy for the Gendlii, and I have lost my top-level access to the programming on the shell."

Reg looked abashed. "I-I didn't mean for you . . . you shouldn't have to—"

"Don't worry about it," said Bertoran with a wave of his hand. "Since the program is frozen, it's not such an honor. If you keep this up, pretty soon you'll have the whole set."

"That's the plan," answered Picard. For several minutes, they discussed preparations for the upcoming test. Then exhaustion began to overcome everyone from the away team, including Captain Picard.

"I think we'll leave you to your work now," said the captain with a yawn. "Mr. Barclay, Counselor Troi, I'm sure you need sleep as badly as I do."

"Yes, sir." Reg nodded with relief.

Back in the turbolift, the captain looked with interest at the three crystal shards hanging from Reg's neck. "Are they heavy?"

"You know, sir, they are. But I'm just so glad to be back in gravity, I don't care."

The captain gave him a weary smile. "I suggest that you take these jewels to engineering and put them through the parts replicator, maximum resolution. Then take the originals to security and put them in a vault. Wear the replicas. Even if they're not exact, no one will know."

"Yes, sir," said Reg glumly. He didn't like having to wear fakes, but he understood the logic behind it. What if something happened to him?

"Don't look so worried," said Deanna Troi. "We're halfway done."

"Yes, I know," muttered Barclay. "But why do I feel like the second half is going to be harder?"

Feeling refreshed from a four-hour sleep and a cup of tea, Captain Picard strolled into sickbay looking for Beverly Crusher. He found the good doctor in the physical therapy room, attending to Keefe Nordine, who was riding a stationary bicycle under the watchful eye of Nurse Ogawa. At least Picard thought it was Nordine. It was difficult to tell, since the vagabond had showered, shaved off his beard, and gotten his long black hair cut a decent length.

"Captain!" called Keefe Nordine with delight. "Look what I'm doing. Dr. Crusher says I'm going to be as good as new!"

"With a lot of therapy," she added. "Hello, Jean-Luc. This is quite a patient you brought me. He was suffering from malnutrition, scurvy, rickets, and several other ailments, in addition to muscle atrophy."

"With that list, you sound like an old sailor," said Picard with a smile.

Nordine wrinkled his youthful face. "I never saw how the Frills could live on a diet of podlings. Thank you for getting me out of there, Captain. I thought I was having a great adventure, but now I see I was half crazy. If there's anything I can do to repay you, just let me know."

"That's good to hear, because there is something." The captain turned to Beverly. "Doctor, can he be released to go back to the surface?"

She considered the question. "It would be better if he stayed put. We've cured his dietary deficiencies and have given him one treatment to rebuild his muscles, but we can't treat him unless he's in gravity."

"Mr. Nordine," said the captain, "do you have any experience with the Yiltern?"

The adventurer nodded. "Yes, I've been to their caves, and I've talked with them a few times. They're peaceable creatures—they live off the lichen."

"How do they communicate?"

"They can work a computer keyboard," answered Nordine. "Cutest thing you ever saw. In fact, they're the only ones on Gemworld who appreciate outside technology. We swapped them an old tricorder for some food. If you're going there, bring some gadgets to trade."

"That's precisely the sort of thing I need to know," said Picard. "That's why I would like you to accompany me to the Yiltern enclave."

"Is that cute Elaysian, Melora, going?"

The captain decided to answer that impertinently phrased question indirectly.

"We have to split up, or we'll never reach all the senior engineers in time." Briefly, the captain told Nordine about the threat of thoron radiation killing everything on Gemworld in less than six days.

Nordine gave a low whistle. "That's on top of the mutant crystal? No wonder you people are pushing yourselves so hard." The impish young man turned to Dr. Crusher and smiled. "Thanks for everything you've done for me, but it looks like I've got to ignore doctor's orders. Captain Picard needs me."

"If you were part of the crew, I could order you to stay in sickbay." Crusher sighed and made a notation on her computer padd. "You won't be harmed going back into low gravity, but you won't get any better."

He shrugged. "I'm just going along for the ride." With difficulty, Nordine started to slide off the bicycle.

"No, you stay here and rest," said the captain, laying a comforting hand on the young man's shoulder. "Dr. Crusher and I have some matters to discuss. I'll come and get you when we're ready to leave."

"I'll take good care of him," promised Ogawa.

Nordine smiled mischievously at the nurse. "How about another massage?"

"He said *rest*," snapped the nurse.

Picard escorted Crusher out of sickbay into the corridor. "What do we have to discuss?" asked the doctor.

"A *chateaubriand* in my quarters. Just enough for two," answered the captain with a smile. "It deserves a good Merlot, but the best I can do is a bottle of sparkling apple juice."

"I'd take a cheeseburger and a glass of water." She smiled warmly at him; then her expression grew bittersweet. "You're worried, aren't you?"

"Yes, I am," he answered in a low voice. "There's so much we don't know about that rift . . . and so much we don't understand about Gemworld. I'd like you to evaluate Troi before we go."

"I've done all I can, Jean-Luc. This isn't my specialty."

"Then look at her as a friend, not a doctor. She seemed all right on the last trip down, but there's something different about her . . . distracted. She fears that she'll lose control again, and that the only thing that will help her is another visit to the Gendlii."

"That's one of the species here, isn't it?"

"Yes, I'll tell you about it over dinner. It's quite remarkable." The captain took the doctor's arm and escorted her into the turbolift. "There are species here that exist nowhere else, that *couldn't* exist anywhere else. We've got to save Gemworld, or the loss will be catastrophic."

After the turbolift door shut, Beverly squeezed his hand. "Let's eat first. You can't save the world on an empty stomach."

"Oh, this feels wonderful!" exclaimed Melora Pazlar as she soared weightlessly to the ceiling of transporter room 3. Reg Barclay clomped nervously after her in his magnetic boots, flailing his arms in the air.

"I thought you would like it here!" he called happily, panting for breath.

"So this is where Tangre Bertoran is working with La Forge and Data?" There was nobody here now, so she bounced over to the nearest auxiliary console and began to explore the readouts. *Is it here?* she wondered.

This was the most likely place, because she would have come here anyway, even if Reg hadn't suggested it after their sleep period.

Searching through Starfleet procedures and nomenclature, and several Elaysian schematics, Melora finally spotted what she was looking for—a tiny footnote in the old Elaysian alphabet. She glanced over her shoulder to see that Reg was still tromping slowly across the room, so she selected the footnote and brought it up on the screen. Sure enough, in the old Elaysian language was a very brief message:

"We have a good alternate plan when they fail. Proceed as we discussed. Take no action but stand ready for my order. The Sacred Protector will prevail."

As she heard Reg's footsteps clomp ever closer, Melora erased the tiny footnote. *The Peer will know I've seen it.* She felt a queasy mixture of dread and guilt. These people were only trying to help Gemworld, yet she was betraying them. Despite their good intentions, they were outsiders. They didn't understand what the shell meant to the inhabitants of Gemworld. She couldn't envision having to shut it down. It was like telling humans to drain their oceans or Vulcans to terraform their deserts. The shell wasn't just a machine that nourished and protected them—it was a link to their past. It was a gift from the Ancients.

For betraying Reg, she felt totally ashamed. If he ever found out, he would never trust her again, and she wouldn't blame him. She faced serious consequences for her actions, but none was so bad as the thought of losing Reg's affection.

For disobeying orders and obstructing a mission, she

could serve ten or twenty years in a Starfleet brig—a tiny cell on a planet full of gravity. That thought was frightening enough, but the realization that she had subverted her oath to Starfleet was worse. Until this moment of betrayal, Melora had never known how important Starfleet was to her.

But Starfleet isn't more important than my own people and my homeworld. Starfleet isn't more important than the Sacred Protector!

Her conflicting emotions erupted in tears, and Melora was caught off guard when Reg effortlessly twisted her weightless body around. "What's the matter?" he asked in alarm.

"I'm . . . I'm just so worried," she lied. "If we fail, there will never be time for me and you."

"M-Me and you?" he asked with surprise and delight. Awkwardly he wrapped his arms around her, and she hugged him back ferociously. With him rooted to the deck and her floating, it was like a newspaper wrapped around a pole in a heavy wind. Melora felt as if she were buffeted by that same wind, tossing her this way and that, sending her careening in directions she had never envisioned.

"You know how I feel about you," she whispered through her tears.

"I guess so," he answered, still sounding amazed. "I could never hope that you felt the same way about me that I . . . I love you, Melora. And we're not going to fail! We've been in some pretty tight spots, I can tell you. If Captain Picard thinks this will work, then it will."

"I love you, too, Reg," she rasped. At least that much was true.

Somehow his mouth found hers, and a tentative kiss grew into a passionate embrace. They clung to each other in the empty space of transporter room 3, one rooted to the deck, the other floating in the air.

"Promise me you'll always love me . . . no matter what," begged Melora.

"I'll love you, no matter what," he answered hoarsely.

They kissed again, longingly, this time with all the pent-up passion that had been building since their arrival on Gemworld. Neither one knew what might happen next, but they could find some refuge from the turmoil and uncertainty in each other's arms.

Melora snuggled into the crook of Reg's neck. "I could stay here all day. Can't you tell the rift, the captain, Tangre Bertoran, and everybody else to just go away? Can't there be any escape for us?"

"Escape is the last thing I want," said Reg. "Maybe we only have six days to live, but I've never been happier in my life!"

His combadge chirped, and Reg reluctantly pushed Melora away to answer it. "Barclay here."

"This is Data," came the response. "Captain Picard requests your presence in his ready room. Is Lieutenant Pazlar with you?"

Reg grinned broadly and held her tighter. "Oh, yes, she's with me."

"Please bring her along. Data out."

The lieutenant gazed fondly at his beloved. "Don't worry, I'll take her everywhere I go."

Melora hugged him again, stifling her tears. She didn't think she could ever betray this wonderful man who only wanted to love her, but she knew she would have to do exactly that, or betray her own people.

"Really, I'm fine," insisted Deanna Troi as she and Beverly Crusher walked slowly down a deserted corridor, headed for the turbolift.

Crusher frowned sternly as only a doctor can. "Of course, 'fine' is a relative term. Captain Picard is worried about you, and so am I."

"Just because I went completely bonkers for a while?" asked Troi cheerfully. "Why would that worry anybody?"

"If it weren't for the circumstances," warned Beverly, "you wouldn't be on active duty. But the captain is right—you have a special rapport with this planet and its inhabitants."

Deanna nodded, gazing directly ahead with an intensity that worried Beverly. "Whatever happens to Gemworld is going to happen to me: our destinies are intertwined. . . . Whatever is attacking her also attacked me."

"What?" asked Beverly, shaking her mane of auburn hair.

The Betazoid stopped in the hallway and gazed at her old friend with dark eyes that were a little too fierce and bright. "Since that first dream, when the Lipuls sent their dreamships for me, my mind has been opened up. It's like I'm a receptor, and I can't control it. There's another being out there—not one of the six sentient species on Gemworld . . . and it's opened up a channel to me. I don't know where it's coming from— it may be the rift—but I do know that it's going to come back."

Crusher didn't like the sound of this. "You think you're going to have more delusions?"

"No, I think this time I'll be able to recognize it and face it," said Troi resolutely. "But if I lose it, take me back to the Gendlii. It's my only hope."

The doctor shook her head, wishing she could commit Troi to sickbay for the duration, but the captain needed her. Maybe this whole damn planet needed her—as she seemed to believe.

"There's the turbolift," said Crusher, pointing to the recessed archway. "Watch out for yourself, please."

"Just remember what I told you," urged Troi as she stepped toward the lift, which opened at her approach. "I'm not insane, I'm just trying to make contact."

"That's what they all say," quipped the doctor with a grudging smile.

As the turbolift doors slid shut, Deanna gave Beverly a reassuring smile, and for a moment the doctor believed that her good friend would be all right.

Then she thought about the possibility of Troi being correct—that an unknown entity lurked on the other side of the rift, making contact through people's dreams . . . and she shivered. All this time, they had been fighting what they thought was a natural disaster, almost a predictable one considering Gemworld's fragile state. If this were an actual attack, it meant war against a Federation planet—possibly a war fought between two different dimensions, with these rifts being the enemy's main weapon. Of course, if the entity could infect their dreams too, then they were helpless.

Crusher shook her head. Maybe she herself was starting to have delusions. Everything around them was so alien that it was difficult to tell what was real and what was illusion. Gemworld itself didn't look as if it should exist, but it did. The dimensional rift didn't exist according to their sensors, yet there it was, bombarding them with darkmatter and thoron radiation. All the might of Starfleet ought to be able to rescue them, but Starfleet was helpless. After the loss of the *Summit,* they would not be sending any more ships into Gemworld's solar system.

They were alone in an alien environment, left to deal with a problem they only half understood. Deanna was not her usual self, and they were dependent upon an insecure midlevel engineer and a bunch of nonhumanoid life-forms they had never encountered before. Her side still had Captain Jean-Luc Picard and the crew of the *Enterprise,* but would that be enough?

With six people present, Captain Picard's ready room was crowded. The captain surveyed the expectant faces: Deanna Troi, Data, Reg Barclay, Melora Pazlar, and Keefe Nordine. He disliked having to depend on a civilian such as Nordine, but the circumstances didn't allow him to be picky. The young man was wearing leg braces and an anti-grav suit similar to the one Pazlar wore. He seemed to be coping with gravity as well as could be expected.

"Thank you all for coming on such short notice," he began. "I trust all of you got a chance to rest and refresh yourselves. We've been very successful in getting cooperation from three senior engineers, but we have three more to go. Since we can't use transporters, and the travel times are so long, I've decided to split our group into two teams—each with its own shuttlecraft."

He pointed to the stalwart android. "Mr. Data and Mr. Nordine will accompany me to the main Yiltern enclave. Commander Troi and Lieutenants Barclay and Pazlar will seek out the Lipul senior engineer. We'll check in with each other every two hours, and plan to rendezvous in Alpusta territory. I don't envision any problems, but I'll feel more comfortable with two teams in this undertaking. Mine will be Team One, and Commander Troi will lead Team Two."

He turned to Barclay. "If anything should happen to Commander Troi, you'll be in command of Team Two."

"Yes, sir!" answered Reg, sounding more charged up than usual.

The captain looked gravely from one face to another. "I don't need to tell you that there is no room for failure. La Forge assures me that we'll be able to power the shell's forcefields from the *Enterprise,* but we must have all six crystal keys in order to shut down the shell."

Barclay cleared his throat and held up a tentative hand. "Should we . . . should we take the keys by force if necessary?"

"No. That's another reason to have two teams—in case one fails, the other can try. Data has already equipped two shuttlecraft and programmed in the coordinates we'll need. I'd like to leave in fifteen minutes. Any other questions?"

Keefe Nordine held up his hand. "After we solve this problem, where are we going next? Back to Earth?"

The captain smiled and patted the young man on the shoulder. "Don't worry, Mr. Nordine, I will personally make sure that you get home. In the meantime, I've entered you on the duty roster as a civilian mission specialist."

The young adventurer beamed. "Great!"

"I'll see you all in shuttlebay one in fifteen minutes. Dismissed."

Deanna Troi felt very much like a third wheel as she watched Barclay and Pazlar making eyes at each other, slowing down preparations to launch their shuttlecraft. Had Captain Picard noticed their blossoming romance, he might not have put them together on this mission, assuming they would be distracted. But leave it to a man not to notice what was right in front of his face.

She had, of course, known that Reg was smitten with Melora, and now she knew the feelings were reciprocal. The question was, what should she do about it? Both Reg and Melora were integral to the mission— neither one could be replaced—and splitting them up would probably send Barclay into a tizzy. Reg had waited a long time for a romance like this, and she wasn't going to throw cold water on it. Their timing could have been better, but Cupid often struck when you least expected it.

No, thought Troi, *I'll just have to play chaperone and hope for the best.* They were both professionals, and Melora had too much at stake to be distracted. At least that's what Troi was counting on. As for Reg, he was flighty under the best of circumstances, but Melora's presence did seem to make him more responsible. Their mission to Gemworld had already brought out a streak of heroism in Reg that she had seldom seen.

Of course, they might conceivably have reservations about working under a commanding officer who had been hallucinating only a few days ago.

Deanna felt she had recovered, except for the loss of her empathy. She could no longer sense other people's emotions effortlessly—she had to guess how they felt, like humans did. Now she could see why humans were irritable and frustrated so much of the time; it was difficult dealing with people when their emotions were a mystery.

She looked around, trying not to be irritable. "Reg, I think you want to stow the magnetic boots in the locker before you trip over them."

"Right!" he said cheerfully. He promptly dropped an environmental suit in order to pick up the boots.

Melora smiled fondly at the lanky lieutenant and turned back to her instruments. "Commander Troi," she said, "I think I'll follow the nourishment strands all the way to the surface. It might take a little longer, but I don't want to go to the wrong crystal. Sometimes finding a Lipul can be difficult."

"Use your best judgment," answered Troi. "After we're free of the ship, you can turn off the gravity, too."

"Thank you, sir. I appreciate it."

The comm panel beeped, and Captain Picard's voice broke in. "Team One to Team Two."

"Troi here," she answered from the copilot's seat.

"We're ready for launch. What's your status?"

"We're a few minutes behind you," said Troi charitably. "Go ahead, sir. We'll see you at the Alpusta enclave."

"Remember, I want contact every two hours. Picard out."

Deanna leaned back in her seat. As she looked out the main window at the cavernous shuttlebay, the gigantic hangar doors swept open, revealing the unexpected sight of pale blue sky crisscrossed in the distance by the metal bands of the shell. To starboard, another shuttlecraft lifted off the deck and slowly moved toward the open door, picking up speed as it went. By the time the captain's shuttlecraft, under Data's sure-handed control, cleared the doors, it had turned into a streak.

Troi hoped their slow start wasn't a precursor of things to come, but she didn't feel very lucky. Then again, who knew? With a pair of starry-eyed lovers on her team, maybe the fates would smile kindly on them.

Chapter Seven

CAPTAIN PICARD GAZED OUT the window at a sight that might have inspired Scheherazade and the authors of *One Thousand and One Arabian Nights*. The sky between two immense yellow prisms was dotted with what appeared to be flying carpets, undulating slowly in the breeze. The Yilterns were obviously aware of the shuttlecraft, but they had no desire to get too close or to race the visitors as had the Frills. Instead, these undulating flyers—each of whom was a composite of hundreds of smaller batlike beings— were content to swoop about like manta rays at play.

"Pretty, aren't they?" asked Keefe Nordine behind him.

"Yes," agreed Picard with a satisfied smile. "I saw one of them in the hall of the Exalted Ones, but I haven't seen them since. Do they ever break apart from that composite form?"

"Into individual animals?" asked Nordine. "Only when they die and when they mate. Or so I've heard."

"That is my information, too," answered Data. "Each one of the larger forms is a brood of siblings, consisting of up to three hundred individuals, sharing a hive-mind. When they find another composite Yiltern to mate with, then all the individual creatures must mate individually with their counterparts. It is quite a spectacle, according to reports."

"Then why isn't the planet overrun with Yilterns?" asked Picard. "If they have broods of three hundred."

"Only a small percentage of each brood are fertile," answered Data, "and each of these must trust to chance to find a fertile counterpart, further reducing the odds. Even for the ones who reproduce, not all of their eggs survive. It is analogous to thousands of human sperm being required to fertilize a single egg."

Keefe Nordine stared wistfully out the window. "They were born together, and most of them will die together. If you look closely, you might find an old one with only a few individuals left. There!"

Following his outstretched finger, Picard located a small Yiltern, which he had initially mistaken for a youngster. The composite form of the Yiltern was a unique creature—it was born full-size and shrank dramatically as it got older.

"They fill in to keep a tight formation," said Nordine. "But when more than half of them are dead, the others just sort of split apart and die. Then the Yiltern is no more."

Picard nodded solemnly, thinking it would be like a starship losing half its crew. It would be disheartening to try to continue under such conditions. He was anxious to learn more about these fantastic creatures, and he wished he had more time to study them. Unfortunately, the team's success depended upon getting in and out of here as quickly as possible.

"We are approaching an opening in the crystal," said Data, pointing the nose of the shuttlecraft toward a jagged crevice at the very tip of a dark-amber prism. "Is that the cave you described?"

"Yes!" answered the young man excitedly. "Only it's not really a cave. It takes them centuries, but the Yilterns pick away at a crystal until they open a hole to the marrow. The liquid escapes and condenses on the walls of the cavern they've made, and they bring in lichen from other caves, which they cultivate. That's all they eat. I guess one of the hollowed-out crystals lasts them thousands of years; then they abandon it when it goes dry."

The captain peered more closely, and he thought he saw metal scaffolding erected around the edge of the crevice. "Has somebody helped them drill these holes?"

Nordine smiled. "I told you, they'll make use of alien equipment if they have it. I think this is their main cavern—it was the last time I was here. This whole area is full of their caves, both current and abandoned."

"I do not believe we should fly inside the prism," said Data, "although the opening is large enough."

"How extensive are the caves inside?" asked the captain.

Nordine answered, "They can go back a long way before they connect with the marrow."

"We can use the jetpacks," suggested Data.

Nordine clapped his hands together. "Hey, great! They'll love that."

"One jetpack," corrected the captain. "You wear it, Data, and you can tow Mr. Nordine and myself on a rope. I don't want to disrupt their living space any more than we have to."

"They won't mind," said Nordine with a smile. "Let's not forget the goodies to trade."

"Surplus items." Picard pointed to a cache of small electronic devices in a net bag.

"I hope that will be enough," said the young passenger.

When they neared the opening in the tip of the amber crystal, Data brought the shuttlecraft to a full stop. As soon as the thrusters shut off, they were surrounded by Yilterns flowing all around them, like leaves caught in a dust devil. Several of the remarkable creatures roosted right on the shuttlecraft, and tiny skittering sounds could be heard through the hull.

Data turned his head, looking mildly concerned. "I hope they will not damage the shuttlecraft."

"I think they're inspecting it," said Nordine, grabbing the bag of trading items. "They're really curious critters."

A few minutes later, Data had a small, self-contained jetpack strapped to his back and a length of rope trailing from his waist. Picard had looped himself next in line about four meters behind the android, and Nordine was last on the line about four meters behind Picard.

The captain was more than willing to let the young man take charge of their trading objects.

When they opened the hatch, the Yilterns moved politely away from the craft, not fleeing but undulating slowly like great gray waves rolling off an embankment. When the creatures moved vertically, they looked like shower curtains instead of carpets, rippling gracefully along unseen rails. Picard couldn't help but be reminded of schools of fish he had seen move in perfect formation, each individual keeping its place in the filmy curtain.

"I am ready," said Data, unimpressed by the extraordinary life flowing all around him.

"Take us in," ordered Picard. "Slowly."

Using very short bursts from his jetpack, the android moved slowly toward the gaping crevice, pulling the two humans and the bag of goods after him. Not only had scaffolding and solar panels been erected around the opening, but there was also a sort of miniature laser drill that stood poised to cut the crevice even wider. Picard frowned, because he didn't have anything in his bag quite as efficient as that drill.

Before he could contemplate this further, their momentum carried them inside the crystal and they were surrounded on all sides by shifting, golden sunlight refracted through the amber crystal. However, it seemed darker than it should be—darker than it had been inside any of the other hollow crystals they had visited—and Picard soon understood why. All along the damp walls grew a crusty white lichen, which seemed to glimmer like spun sugar. Although it was beautiful in itself, the lichen cut down on the amount of light reaching the cavern.

As they floated deeper, they disturbed several creatures feeding, who simply peeled off the walls and rippled away. In the shadowy golden half-light Picard saw what he thought were nets, like the ones he had seen in the Elaysian enclaves. Upon closer inspection, he was surprised to find that these nets were wires connected to the hulks of various machines. He was further startled when one of the machines lit up as he passed and an electronic eye regarded him coldly. Despite his certainty that he was inside a large prism, he couldn't shake the feeling that he had entered an alien spacecraft.

The captain noticed a clammy moisture on his face and hands, which he attributed to the condensing marrow of the crystal. The passageway widened to include even more mismatched equipment from various sources, some of it operational. He began to wonder how the Yilterns had gotten the machines in here, when he realized that even the smallest flying creatures could easily move heavy equipment in low gravity.

"Captain," said Data, his voice echoing in the hollow chamber. "I believe we have reached the center."

Data cut the small thrusters on his jetpack, and the three visitors floated into a vast, dimly lit cavern, where dozens—perhaps hundreds—of Yilterns clung to the walls, unmoving. The central feature of the cavern was a jutting chunk of crystal that was capped, like an oil well, with intricate dials, wheels, and nozzles sticking from it. Every few seconds a gust of atomized liquid burst from the capped crystal like a geyser, spewing moisture into the air. So far this was the only place Picard had seen on Gemworld where moisture was not trapped but was allowed some natural evaporation and condensation.

It was eerie inside the clammy cave, with thousands of batlike creatures hanging silently overhead and rows of monitors and discarded equipment blinking enigmatically. The captain wondered how long it would be before their presence was acknowledged and someone came to ask them what they wanted. . . . Perhaps the Yilterns already knew what they wanted.

"We'll have to be patient," Keefe Nordine cautioned him.

"Understood," said the captain. "But my patience has a limit."

Suddenly a complex computer console blinked on, and a scratchy, artificial voice sounded. "Welcome visitors. Please state your business. Are you here to trade?"

"No, not exactly," answered Picard. "We're here to discuss the dimensional rift and what has to be done to stop it."

"Please type your response," said the scratchy voice.

Data at once took over the console, rapidly learning its functions. The captain noticed a bundle of wires stretching upward from the terminal to the highest reaches of the cavern, where more lights glowed intermittently. The way the lights blinked on and off, he had the feeling that several Yilterns were hovering over them.

"I have asked if the senior engineer is present," explained the android.

Picard nodded. "Good thinking."

"Leave it to an android to cut right to the chase," said Nordine. "But you should know that they don't respond well to high-pressure sales tactics."

Like a parachute dropping slowly through the atmosphere, a large Yiltern floated toward them from above. The edges of the creature fluttered as if caught in the wind, and Picard marveled to see they were really tiny wings, flapping as fast as a hummingbird's wings. The creature seemed to be making for the terminal, and Data moved back to allow it access.

Like a blanket, the Yiltern completely covered the computer console. Picard pressed closer, and saw that what looked like a seamless blanket was in reality a teeming mass of tiny batlike animals. They swarmed over the terminal, pressing membranes and switches, and the artificial voice responded. "He is coming."

Undulating like a wave, the Yiltern picked itself up from the console and flew over their heads, settling on the bag of trade goods. In a flash, the net bag was completely engulfed by the squirming mass of tiny beings.

"That's a good sign," said Nordine. "They're inspecting the merchandise."

"Captain," said Data, pointing back toward the entrance of the cave.

Picard turned around in time to see a small Yiltern come undulating slowly toward them, towing what appeared to be a clump of gaily colored ribbons. The fact that this being was small meant that it was old and probably highly respected. Picard hoped it was the senior engineer.

· The small being stopped at the bag full of trade goods, and the first creature peeled off and backed away. The smaller Yiltern let go of its cargo, and the clump of ribbons floated in the air while it inspected the bagful of trade goods.

Trying not to appear too curious, Picard edged closer to the creature. He really wanted to see what was in that gaily wrapped package more than he wanted to see the Yiltern. Something shiny caught his eyes, and he thought he saw the glimmer of a facet in the midst of all those ribbons. He realized that each ribbon might be carried in the mouth of an individual, so that all of them would share in the transportation of this valuable object. With sadness, he realized there were many more ribbons than individual beings left in the aged Yiltern.

As if sensing that the visitor had gotten too close to the prize, the small Yiltern suddenly peeled away from the bag, snatched the clump of ribbons, and flew upward into the shadows. Until that moment, Picard hadn't realized the composite beings could move so quickly.

"Have I offended it?" he asked Nordine.

The young man shrugged. "I don't know. But maybe you showed too much interest."

Shadows flitted across the ceiling of the vast cavern, and it was evident that some kind of discussion was taking place above their heads. Once again, Picard fought the temptation to be demanding. *When in Rome,* he kept telling himself, *do as the Romans do.*

Finally the Yilterns settled back onto their roosts and the disconcerting shadows stopped moving overhead. The computer terminal blinked awake, and the artificial voice said, "You want something of great value."

Picard pointed to the keyboard. "Data, tell them how important this is. But briefly."

The android fell upon the keyboard and typed briskly. When he was done, there was a faint chirping sound from somewhere in the amber shadows, and the geyser spewed a cloud of clammy mist.

The voice said dully, "We know. Still you want something of great value."

Picard mustered a smile. "As you can see, we have brought with us various items from our ship. We'll be happy to leave these with you as a token of—"

"We want the shuttlecraft."

Picard stopped in midsentence, realizing that they couldn't hear him anyway. His lips thinned, and he looked at Data, who immediately rechecked the computer.

"Their request is broken down in greater detail on this screen," reported the android. "They do require the shuttlecraft. In addition, they have accounted for most of our on-board inventory, which they are also claiming as collateral."

"Collateral?" asked Picard. "Does that mean we'll get it back if we return the crystal?"

"Unknown, sir."

"I suggest you take this deal, Captain," said Nordine. "For something of value they want something of value. That's the way they look at things."

The captain frowned and pointed at Data. "They don't get all of it. We keep the jetpacks, our two phaser pistols, and our tricorders—whatever we can carry."

"Yes, sir," answered Data, leaning over the terminal. "I will tell them we need basic items for survival."

"Boy, Captain, you drive a hard bargain," said Nordine with a grin.

Picard scowled. "Just be thankful they didn't ask for *you.*"

When the comm signal sounded, Deanna Troi stopped floating leisurely in the cabin of her shuttlecraft and pushed herself into her seat. She checked the chronometer to make sure it wasn't time for another check-in, and it wasn't. This had to be an emergency.

"Away Team Two," she answered. "Troi here."

"Picard here," came a gruff response. "We've been successful, but we had to give up our shuttlecraft as part of the bargain."

Melora Pazlar snorted a laugh, but she kept her eyes on the nourishment strand they'd been following for hours. Troi gathered that the Elaysian had half-expected something like that would happen.

"Understood, sir," answered Deanna. "Do you want us to come and get you?"

"No, we'll contact the *Enterprise* for another shuttle. Your first priority is to get the key from the Lipuls. Take down our coordinates. If you finish quickly, you can come get us, and I'll cancel the other shuttle. We've got our jetpacks, so we're still mobile, but slow. I wanted you to know that we can't be of much assistance to you."

"Understood, sir."

"Team One out."

Troi flicked off the signal and leaned back in her seat. The concerned face of Reg Barclay floated overhead. "What does that mean? Are they stranded?"

"Apparently so. It just means we're on our own." Troi glanced at Pazlar. "What are you smiling about?"

"Outsiders often get out-bargained by the Yilterns," she answered. "They're the closest thing we have to Ferengi."

"Why didn't you warn the captain?" asked Troi.

"He has his guide, Mr. Nordine," she answered brusquely. "Just be glad you have me."

"We are glad," said Reg sincerely.

"How much farther?" asked Troi, losing a bit of her infinite patience.

"Until this strand reaches the engineer's base prism," answered Pazlar. "It should be soon. I just didn't want to lose it."

Reg moved closer to Melora. "Is that strand the only way the Lipuls have to get to and from the shell?"

"Right," she answered. To her credit, Melora had stopped looking lovesick the moment she put her hands on the controls of the shuttlecraft. If she had any interest in Reg, it was only as a somewhat talkative passenger in her shuttlecraft.

She peered intently out the window, as if they were about to encounter something significant. "These are the right coordinates," said Melora. "Commander Troi, put the sensors on that pale blue crystal at ten o'clock. See if there are any life-signs."

"Okay." For the sixth time in their journey, Troi ran a scan of a large old-growth prism. This one was a dull icy blue, although it was striated with disturbing blotches of black mutant crystal. Deanna didn't know why, but she had envisioned something grander. This didn't look like the kind of prism where a senior engineer would live. It seemed old, cracked, diseased—far past its prime—although it was still gargantuan.

"No life-signs yet," she reported after surveying the readings.

"Hmmm," grumbled Pazlar. "That's odd. Look . . . the strand ends here."

Sure enough, it was plain to see as they circled the old blue monolith that the nourishment strand they had been following for the better part of a day did indeed go no farther. After an impossibly long chain of prisms, the strand nourished this last monolith, and the cluster it was part of, then ended in a severed stump.

"So it's got to be here?" asked Troi.

Melora scowled. "If it's not here, then where is it? Lipuls can't fly. They have to swim."

"Did we pass it by . . . somewhere?" asked Reg with concern.

"Let's stop and look with tricorders," said Pazlar. "If that's okay with you, Commander?"

Troi nodded. "Go ahead."

For the first time, she had to consider a possibility that seemed absurd—that they wouldn't be able to secure the Lipuls' crystal because they couldn't find the Lipul. Until now, Troi hadn't realized how insane it was to look for a single Lipul in a haystack of giant prisms. But if they had miscalculated, or if the senior engineer were trying to stay hidden from them, they might be in for a long, tough search. Lipuls lived isolated lives. There was no enclave in which to seek them.

Pulling horizontally alongside the giant blue prism, the shuttlecraft fired thrusters and came to a stop about ten meters from the nearest facet. Up close,

Deanna could see what awful damage the mutant crystal was wreaking on this once-proud monolith. It looked blighted and dry, as if the life had been sucked out of it.

Melora popped the hatch and was the first one out, tricorder in hand. She moved effortlessly in the low gravity, letting her billowy white gown catch the breeze and propel her slowly to the edge of the prism. Deanna waited until Reg had a chance to push off the shuttle and drift after her, and she noted that he was moving more gracefully in low gravity. She made sure the shuttle's communications were patched into her combadge, then she grabbed her own tricorder and flew out the hatch.

Troi caught up with her companions at the blue wall of the monolith. Faintly through the thick crystal, they could see bubbles moving the length of the prism.

"If there's no gravity," said Reg, "what causes the current to move in the crystals?"

"Transpiration," answered Melora, not taking her eyes off her tricorder. "It's the same thing that makes water flow up a tree trunk on Earth. A liquid just naturally seeks dryness. The bubbles move with changes in the pressure."

Barclay stared at his tricorder. "Thoron radiation is awfully high here. Do you read that?"

"Yes," said Melora, her forehead ridges deepening. "If it gets much higher, we'll have to put on the suits."

Deanna was frowning as grimly as Melora, as she pushed herself away from the giant blue prism. She wanted to see the entire prism, because she had a sickening feeling that they were going to spend hours—

perhaps days—searching this thing with tricorders. That would be slow, tedious, and probably fruitless.

With relative ease, Troi reached the shuttlecraft and was about to push off again, when she saw a shadow moving along the length of the pale blue monolith. At least it appeared to be a shadow, although nothing large was moving in the sky. *What could cast a moving shadow?* As the Betazoid looked more closely, she realized that it was in reality a dark mass, like a clot, moving *inside* the crystal. It was in the marrow stream.

"Pazlar. Look at this." Deanna motioned for the others to join her, while never taking her eyes off the slow-moving clot. Both Melora and Reg tagged up on the crystal and pushed off, with Melora reaching the shuttlecraft a moment before Reg. The Elaysian held out her hand and caught the lanky lieutenant, bringing him safely to a rung on the hatch.

Now all three of them could see the black bruise beneath the translucent crystal, and could also see that it was moving closer to them. The Elaysian gasped aloud. "Just like in my dream! It's my *dream!*"

Troi wasn't entirely sure what she meant, and she reacted slowly when Melora ducked into the shuttlecraft and emerged a moment later. She didn't realize that Pazlar was holding one of their two phaser pistols until she aimed it at the oncoming apparition and fired.

"Pazlar! *Don't!*" shouted Troi.

But it was too late. With her phaser set to full, the wild-eyed Elaysian was drilling a burning red hole in the crystal just ahead of the shadow. Deanna reached for Melora, and so did Reg, but neither one of them wanted to grab a phaser spitting a red beam at full intensity. They were helpless to stop her as she opened a hole in the path of the dark clot. Smoke, powder, and chips of crystal flew everywhere until she had finally drilled straight into the marrow. Milky liquid spewed out like a geyser, and the black mass kept coming at its inexorable pace.

"That's enough!" shouted Troi.

Pazlar lowered the weapon and motioned to the shuttlecraft. "Get inside! Now!"

The hole was widening under the pressure of the escaping liquid, and the blue facet was beginning to crack. Getting inside the shuttlecraft seemed like a very good idea. Both Barclay and Troi moved like Elaysians as they grabbed the struts and rungs and hauled themselves inside. Melora gave them a final shove, sending them to the rear of the craft, then she hurriedly shut the hatch behind her.

"Putting up shields," said Pazlar, working the instrument panel.

Troi wanted to chew her out for her rash action, but she couldn't tear her eyes away from the sight of the icy blue surface breaking apart and spewing liquid that was becoming increasingly darker, and flecked with black and brown globs. Swiftly, the discolored clot surged toward the opening and the prism erupted with a vicious gush, pouring outward what looked like all the filth and wretchedness of the universe.

Deanna felt herself getting light-headed, and she struggled to maintain her consciousness. *I am in control!* she told herself. *My mind belongs to me!*

As the torrent of mutant marrow sizzled against their shields, all three of them cringed. Troi tried to tell herself that this wasn't the enemy, this was just his waste product, just his weaponry. If she couldn't face this, she couldn't face any of it—she was useless.

With an effort Troi breathed calmly and evenly, trying to remember her yoga training. *This will pass. My inner strength will guide me.* Although it seemed to take a lifetime, the dark sludge finally stopped spewing from the wound in the great prism, and Deanna felt the cloud lift from her mind.

She looked up, to see that they were surrounded by globules of murky liquid floating listlessly all around the shuttlecraft. More discharge oozed from the hole in the crystal facet, but the pressure had equalized.

"Pazlar, you are relieved of duty," she said calmly.

"But I had to! Didn't you see it—" The Elaysian continued to protest loudly, but Deanna ignored her.

"Barclay, get on the sensors."

"Y-Yes, sir!" responded the lieutenant, hopping into the copilot's seat. "W-What are we looking for?"

"A Lipul—anything organic . . . the crystal key."

Melora regarded her intently. "There wasn't time to get your permission. I had to act. *You* wouldn't have destroyed the crystal—it had to be me."

"We'll discuss this later," snapped Troi. "And if you don't shut up I'll have you thrown into the brig when we get back to the *Enterprise.*"

Pazlar flew to the rear of the cabin and curled in a corner, sulking.

"I . . . um, I think I found something," reported Barclay. "It's something organic."

Deanna hovered over his shoulder, looking down at the tiled windows, which rapidly pinpointed the object on the sensors. They continued to zoom in until a grainy image formed amid the murky liquid floating near the prism.

"Increase magnification," said Troi.

Barclay obeyed, and the image jumped to a larger size and took over the screen. It still looked like just another globule, until Reg clarified the resolution. Troi felt Melora Pazlar hovering over her shoulder, but she didn't tell the Elaysian to go away. She deserved to see the image that was forming on the screen.

Floating amidst the marrow from the crystal was a shriveled corpse about the size and shape of a jellyfish.

Chapter Eight

FROM A SAFE DISTANCE, Captain Picard, Commander Data, and Keefe Nordine watched the Yilterns swarm all over their shuttlecraft. As the odd creatures flowed in and out of the hatch, they looked like packing blankets shifting in the wind.

The captain glanced around nervously. He felt exposed, floating in the open between two giant prisms that stretched into the sky. However, he could think of no reason why they would be in danger, now that they had lost most of their belongings. As usual, the biggest danger was of wasting time, but there seemed to be no way to avoid that. He tried to tell himself that they had made good progress and were ahead of schedule for securing the six crystal keys. But it was hard to be cheerful when one's only means of transportation had been taken over by the locals.

"Do you really think they'll try to fly it?" asked Nordine curiously.

Data cocked his head. "I would presume so, judging by the fact that they appear to use most of the equipment they have procured."

"Can they do it?" asked Nordine.

"They showed considerable manual dexterity in operating their computers," answered the android. "If they can comprehend the concepts and basic operation, I see no reason why they cannot pilot a shuttlecraft. They are at least as intelligent as a first-year Starfleet cadet."

"More, I'd say," replied Nordine with a wry grin.

"I take it you don't think much of Starfleet?" asked Picard.

"Did I say that?" The young man looked abashed. "You have to have connections to get into Starfleet, plus good grades, and I never had either."

The captain scratched his chin, thinking that Nordine had become more pensive and serious since their encounter with the Gendlii, although he occasionally reverted to his flippant attitude. The young man probably just needed some encouragement and direction.

"You have the prime requisites for Starfleet," said Picard, "an urge to explore and a sense of adventure. I'd hate to think we're going to fix your legs and take you all the way back to Earth just so you can turn around and get lost on another harebrained lark."

The young man grimaced. "A 'harebrained lark'? You wound me, Captain. Believe me, I've had enough harebrained larks for a while."

Although he feigned indifference, Nordine cast a sidelong glance at the veteran captain. "Do you really think I could make it in Starfleet?"

"I know that you showed considerable character holding up under your experience with the Frills. You'd need all that and more to get through the academy, especially with your wild streak."

Nordine smiled. "More courage than good sense, right?"

"Courage is a necessary trait in a Starfleet officer," concluded Data. "Unfortunately, there is no accurate way to assess courage until an individual is observed under stressful conditions. I would concur—you possess more courage than good sense."

Nordine laughed and patted the android on the shoulder. "Why, thank you, Data!"

"You are welcome." In a low voice, Data added, "By the way, if you require 'connections,' the captain has them."

"I'm sure he does."

A chirp sounded on the captain's combadge and he frowned, thinking it wasn't time for anyone to report in again. "Away Team One," he answered.

"This is Troi with Team Two," came a familiar voice. "Captain, we've had a bit of a setback. We found the Lipul senior engineer, but it was dead."

"Dead?" asked Picard in shock. "Inside its prism?"

"Yes. As far as we can tell, the mutant crystal invaded the marrow and somehow smothered the Lipul. We don't know for sure. If you saw how huge this prism is, you would think the Lipuls could have evaded it, but who knows?"

Picard said, "I want you to preserve the body in a stasis field and take it back to Crusher for an autopsy."

"Yes, sir, we've preserved it."

"What about the crystal key?"

"There's no sign of it," answered Troi, "although it could be anywhere inside this gigantic prism. We have Barclay's keys, and we've input their patterns into our tricorders to see if we can use them to locate the missing one. I can't give you a timetable, sir, but we can't take the Lipul back to the ship as long as we're searching here."

The captain scowled, thinking that he'd had just about enough of setbacks and bizarre delays. Also, he didn't like the idea that two of the senior engineers had shown up mysteriously dead—first the Elaysian and now the Lipul. They had four of the six shards they needed, but those last two might prove impossibly difficult to get.

"Sir?" asked Troi with alarm. "Are you there, sir?"

"Yes, I was just thinking," replied the captain. "We've sent for another shuttlecraft, but it won't be here for about seven hours. It sounds like you need our help, and we need yours. How far away from us are you?"

There was a pause, and Troi answered, "You seem to be about four hundred kilometers away, as the crow flies."

"We've got jetpacks, so we can fly like crows," replied Picard. "Data, have we got a range of four hundred kilometers on these jetpacks?"

"With the absence of gravity, they have a range of 672 kilometers," answered the android. "At a constant speed of seventy kilometers per hour."

Picard concluded, "We can reach you on our jet-packs, and then all of us can search for the shard. Commander Troi, start the homing signal on the shuttlecraft."

"Yes, sir."

"Data, can you track it?"

"Yes, sir." The android swiveled his head, stopping every few centimeters like a satellite dish looking for a signal. "I have it, sir."

"We'll be there as quickly as we can," concluded the captain. "Picard out."

"Sir," said Data, "we will be exposed to broken crystal and gravity spikes as we travel."

"We're exposed to them while we stay here and wait," replied the captain. "I'd rather keep moving."

"Let's say good-bye to the shuttlecraft," suggested Nordine. By the swirl of activity around the small craft, it looked as if the Yilterns were about to drag it off.

The captain scowled, still angry about losing the shuttle, even if only temporarily. He took the controls of his jetpack in hand and looked at his young companion. "Mr. Nordine, you said you knew how to fly one of these things."

"For an old daredevil like me, this is nothing." Nordine looked confident as he put his hands on the dual controls and squared his shoulders. "Lead the way, Data!"

"Follow me." The android applied thrusters and zoomed off, his body at right angles to the amber prism of the Yilterns. Keefe Nordine soared into line behind him, and Captain Picard brought up the rear, careful to keep about twenty meters' clearance.

It felt exhilarating to be flying in the open air, soaring over the majestic crystals and into the vast expanse of shimmering sky. Without gravity to overcome, the slightest thruster burst gave great acceleration, and Picard found that he could cruise along on a minimum of fuel. As he had no instruments to watch, he found he could keep his eyes glued on Nordine and Data as they swooped and soared among the lofty prisms.

Ahead of him, he heard the young man howl with delight.

Flying this way was entirely too much fun, and Picard had to remind himself that this was serious business. They skirted a clump of black crystals floating in a sooty cloud, and Picard reminded himself that it was also dangerous business. Nevertheless, they were soon soaring through open skies again, and the smile crept back on the captain's face.

With a scowl, Commander Will Riker surveyed the circular bridge of the *Enterprise,* muttering under his breath about the weird dreams and strange circumstances that had brought them to Gemworld. He particularly disliked having to maneuver so close to a huge object like the shell when he didn't have Data to help him navigate. It wasn't that he lacked faith in his young bridge crew, many of whom had been tested during the Dominion War, but he missed having the first team, which included Data, Deanna, and Captain Picard.

Now the captain had sent word that he didn't need the second shuttlecraft he had requested. Unless his situation had changed, that meant that he, Data, and the civilian were zooming around Gemworld on jetpacks with no protection and no security. Riker had lost countless battles to keep the captain away from perilous situations, but this had seemed more like a diplomatic mission. . . . He hadn't even fought it. Now he was wondering if he shouldn't have insisted on more personnel, more shuttlecraft . . . more *something*.

In his pacing, Riker passed a screen showing a view of the brightly colored world beneath them. To him, Gemworld looked like the colored rock candy they used to sell at an antique shop near his home in Valdez, Alaska. That candy had been pretty to look at, but when you tried to eat it, it was stale and brittle. He felt that way about Gemworld—pretty to the eye, but insipid to the taste.

"Commander," called the tactical officer. "We're being hailed by Tangre Bertoran. They're ready for us to take our position."

With a sigh, Riker took his seat in the command chair. "Course laid in?"

"Yes, sir, course laid in," answered the conn.

"Proceed at one-fourth impulse." He settled back in his seat and watched the screen, trying not to think how unsettling it was to be poking along in the atmosphere of a planet. This big bird needed to be in black space, not blue sky. But there it was—blue sky as far as he could see, except for the distant bands of the shell.

"Seven hundred kilometers and closing," reported the ops station.

"Be prepared to drop shields at one hundred."

"Yes, sir."

He hated having to drop shields, but that was the

whole point of this exercise. They had to get close enough to the shell to be protected by its forcefields, if they hoped to keep those same forcefields working when the shell was turned off.

Riker sat forward nervously. "Any gravity spikes or floating debris?"

"No, sir, the route appears to be clear," answered ops. "Five hundred kilometers and closing."

Riker still refused to relax. "No life-forms in the area?"

"There are some Alpusta off to port, leaving the shell, but we won't intercept them."

"Hold steady."

"Three hundred kilometers." The seconds ticked away in Riker's mind, while the metallic bands on the viewscreen began to solidify behind the clouds, making the sky look fake, like part of a holodeck scene. *Unnatural place,* he thought.

"One hundred kilometers, dropping shields," reported ops. "Thoron radiation within tolerance level."

"One-eighth impulse," ordered Riker.

He frowned as they drew closer and closer to the alien machine, with its kidney-shaped pools of space—like keyholes into the unknown. Although they had docked at numerous starbases in their time, a starbase was always a clearly defined object floating in space. With this thing, it looked as if they were about to plow into a fence. It wasn't until they were close enough to count the potholes and broken antennas that they finally stopped.

"Coordinates achieved," reported the Bolian on the conn. "Full stop."

"Well done," said Riker, as everyone on the bridge relaxed and glanced at one another with relief.

"The shell is hailing," reported tactical.

"On screen."

The beaming face of the white-haired Peer of the Jeptah appeared on the viewscreen. Tangre Bertoran was floating among other yellow-garbed Jeptah, holding his arms open; they looked like a heavenly choir.

"Perfect, Commander Riker!" declared the Elaysian. "I told you it would not be difficult. Now we can proceed with the rest of our experiment."

"So do you want to go ahead and put us under your forcefield?" asked Riker.

Bertoran shrugged. "If we don't, you are vulnerable to mutant crystal floating loose."

"All right, but we still have twenty-four hours until the transfer test."

"Of course," answered Tangre Bertoran with a smile. "Commander La Forge assures me that the test will be fine. 'Piece of cake,' I think he said. Whatever that means."

"Commander," said the Deltan on ops, "there are a large number of Alpusta exiting the shell."

Riker shifted uncomfortably in his seat. "What's that all about?"

"It's nothing," said Bertoran. "Just their shift change. If you're worried about contact with workers coming and going, let us put you under our forcefield. Feel secure, the Holy Protector has guarded Gemworld for countless millions of your years, and it will guard you."

"Right," said Riker, thinking it was inevitable. If they hoped to hold this planet-sized ball of air together, they would have to give up the power they were diverting to their shields.

"All right. Should we do anything special?"

"You have some residual forcefields in various parts of your ship," answered Bertoran. "You may want to cancel them, as they will interfere with ours."

Riker frowned. "Those are secure bulkheads and sensitive systems. We don't really turn them off, you know—sort of like the shell."

"Very humorous," said Bertoran with a curled lip. "I can't predict the outcome if you leave those small shields active."

The human shrugged good-naturedly. "That's why this is a test. Come on, we need to have our sensitive systems functioning normally. Just see if your forcefield will swallow us whole or not."

"Very well." Bertoran nodded to one of his minions hovering over a monitor.

"Increased protonic discharge," said the ops officer. She suddenly sat bolt upright in her chair, and then slumped over.

In that same instant, Riker's entire body lurched uncontrollably in a spasm of pain and his spine stiffened like a rod. His hand crashed down on the control panel in the arm of his chair, and with his last conscious effort he grunted, *"Computer . . . lock out!"*

Chapter Nine

AS REG BARCLAY FUMBLED clumsily in his bulky environmental suit, he found himself getting more and more twisted and stuck in a hole in the icy-blue crystal. *Curses!* Just when he'd been moving somewhat gracefully in the low gravity of Gemworld, they had to wind up in this motherlode of thoron radiation! Since Melora had ruptured the aged blue crystal and spilled its rancid marrow, they had been inundated with the stuff. All around them, globules and soggy clouds of mutant crystal floated like yesterday's coffee grinds.

Reg looked back sorrowfully at the solitary figure of Melora Pazlar, floating like refuse under the struts of the shuttlecraft. Troi had relieved her of duty, and not without cause. She had acted on her own, rashly, with total disregard for her comrades and the mission. But he still loved Melora. Where she was weak, he was strong; where he was weak, she was strong. The damned thing was, neither one of them had any inter-personal skills. Deanna Troi was about as well-adjusted as a person could be, and if you couldn't get along with her, you were pathetic.

"Come on, Barclay! Get back to work!" ordered Commander Troi in his earphone.

"Y-Yes, sir," he sputtered. "I m-mean . . . n-no, sir!"

"What do you mean, you mean 'no, sir'?"

"I mean . . . request permission to speak frankly with you." Reg pushed himself out of the hole with great effort in order to peer inside the prism, where Troi had already begun the search. Amid the disgusting globs floating about, he spotted her globular white environ-mental suit. "Commander, let's talk."

She spun around in the weightless half-air, half-gel innards of the dying prism. Although Melora had sounded the death-knell for this old-growth monolith, it had been fading already. The disease had gotten to it, reminding Reg of a giant saguaro cactus he had seen in Arizona, speckled black and disintegrating from the blight. Troi's body floated in the distance like some an-gelic bird in the midst of the rotting carcass of a once proud giant.

"I'm listening," said Troi with resignation.

"I know I'm not entirely unbiased," said Reg, "but these are special circumstances. Melora is the only one of us who lives here; she feels what happens here more deeply than we do. Commander Troi, they told me that you went completely . . . um, well, that you had prob-lems with . . . you know—"

"I was delirious," said Troi bluntly. "You think that because Captain Picard gave me another chance, I should give Melora another chance."

Reg nodded eagerly. "Please!"

The distant white figure waved her arms. "Reg, you're in *love* with her! You have no idea what you're talking about."

"That's true," he agreed. "But I know it will take us a lot longer to search this prism with *two* people instead of *three*. And I know that neither you nor I can fly that shuttlecraft around this cockeyed planet."

Troi's arms dropped to her side. "The captain and Data are joining us."

"In several hours. And when they get here, what are you going to tell them? We would have had to drill a hole into this prism anyway. She saved us hours of work! We're looking for a needle in a haystack."

"All right," Troi sighed. "Let's rendezvous back at the shuttlecraft."

Barclay let out a wheezing breath, which whooshed loudly in the amplified confines of his headgear. *One down, one to go. Now if I can just get through to Melora.*

Five minutes later, all three of them were back at the shuttlecraft, and Troi motioned Pazlar into the hatch. A couple of minutes later, they were floating inside the cabin, and Reg and Deanna took their headgear off. From her perch on the pilot's seat, Melora stared sullenly at them.

Reg threw up his hand. "Commander Troi, may I talk first?"

"Yes, go ahead," said the commander.

The gangly lieutenant took a deep breath, then he began, "The two of you are the only reason we're here. The *Enterprise* would be cruising along nicely, performing important science experiments, if you two hadn't started having those dreams. Now we're here trying to save this ancient planet, and there's no room for error."

Reg turned to Melora and pointed his finger at her. "You have to trust us! The crew of the *Enterprise* is the best we have, and we're willing to sacrifice ourselves for your planet. The Jeptah are too close to this thing to do it without help. Trust me, Melora, I wouldn't lie to you. This crew can save your planet, if you let them."

She lowered her eyes but said nothing.

Reg pointed back at the prism. "The Lipuls knew that nobody but Starfleet could save them, because they knew that this . . . this *darkness* had infected the planet. But the two of you . . . you're the keys to it."

Deanna nodded slowly, and Melora looked down at her feet. Reg waved his hands at both of them, urging them to talk.

It was the Elaysian who spoke first. "I really don't know what came over me, except a certainty that I had to break the crystal and free it . . . even though it was already dead. I apologize, Commander."

"Do you think you can control this rashness in the future?" asked Troi.

"I'd be lying if I said I know what I'm going to do," answered Melora, twisting her hands together. "I'm scared. My homeworld is crumbling all around me. I don't know whom to believe." She smiled fondly at Barclay. "I know I can trust Reg. But I don't know the rest of you very well. Frankly, at the moment, even my own people seem like strangers to me."

Deanna sighed. "That's not exactly the stirring vote of confidence I would have liked, but it will do for now. All right, Pazlar, you're back on duty, and nothing will be said about your actions. But there are no third chances."

"Understood, sir."

Barclay clapped his hands together. "Now all we have to do is think like a Lipul."

"What do you mean, think like a Lipul?" asked Melora.

Reg pointed back at the weathered blue monolith and then at the stasis canister at his feet. "This Lipul was the same one who *told* us to shut down the shell and be ruthless about it. It wasn't hiding from *us*—it came here hiding from something else . . . something that got it, anyway. It had no reason to hide the crystal key from us—you would think that we're *supposed* to find it."

"Do you think it left us a clue?" asked Troi, leaning forward.

"Maybe, but how would a Lipul leave a clue?"

"In a dream," answered Melora softly. "I think we should go back to sleep." The Elaysian turned and looked intently at Deanna Troi.

"A dream that would outlive death?" asked Reg doubtfully.

"It's how they keep their history," said Deanna with realization. "They pass dreams along to one another for safekeeping. They may die, but their dreams don't."

While Reg thought about that, Troi moved swiftly toward the hatch. "The two of you will sleep in here. I'll sleep outside."

Reg stared at her, his mouth gaping. He felt Melora move a hair's breadth closer to him. "But, sir—" he protested.

Troi winked at the two lieutenants. "Take it. This may be your only chance to be alone. That's an order."

"Thank you, Commander," said Melora with gratitude.

"Sweet dreams." Troi dashed outside, shutting the hatch behind her.

Melora drifted across the cabin into his arms, her head nestling in the crook of his shoulder. Although he could hold her warm, trembling body, she had no weight, so it was like holding a mirage . . . a dream. Reg suddenly began to worry that none of this was real—it was all surreal! *What if I wake up and find out that I'm dreaming?*

Her lips answered his doubts. Their bodies meshed, swirling and floating in the cocoon of the shuttlecraft.

Will Riker drew a rasping, painful breath and felt as if he were rising to the surface from very deep in the ocean. That he could breathe at all meant he was wearing an aqualung, although he couldn't remember going scuba diving. He couldn't remember much of anything—only the immediate reality of swimming . . . weightless . . . with his head hurting and his vision clouded. He felt so lousy that for a moment he panicked, thinking he had the bends. It felt as if there were bubbles inside his body, moving the wrong way, poisoning his blood!

So he stopped rising to the surface and tried to swim in place. *If I have the bends, I'm a dead man, anyway,* he realized. Will felt dead—drugged, buried. If only his head didn't hurt so much, maybe he could remember what he was doing here. *Was I underwater and blacked out?*

He tried to open his eyes, but his eyelids felt so thick and heavy—it was as if the water pressed against them, blurring his vision. So he swam in place, breathing raggedly, trying to ignore the pounding in his head. Riker had to be underwater, because there were fish swimming about, one gigantic crablike creature in particular on long stilted legs, and a nasty-looking moray eel. They were upside-down.

As he tried to focus his eyes, the scene became clearer, but more bizarre. He was underwater in a shipwreck ... the wreck of a starship! It looked like the bridge—upside-down and populated by fish, but it was the bridge ... with the blinking consoles and omniscient viewscreens he knew so well. With a start, he realized he was diving in the sunken wreck of the *Enterprise!*

How had this happened? Will wracked his brain, but he had no memory of this crash. Only ... he remembered the *Enterprise* was nowhere near water. It was in the air—the blue sky—which was almost as strange. But Will clearly remembered seeing the ship in his mind's eye, cruising through blue sky, even though that was impossible. He flashed back on the earlier crash of the *Enterprise-D,* but this was not that ship. This was the *E* ... in blue sky.

His eyes widened, and he screamed ... a raw, piercing, primal scream of horror.

Riker stared, wild-eyed. He almost wished he hadn't remembered where he was, and he wished his vision had remained cloudy. It *was* the bridge of the *Enterprise,* only it wasn't submerged underwater. He floated helplessly upside-down, his arms and legs bound tightly, while nightmarish creatures manned the stations on *his* bridge. The thing that looked like a giant moray eel twisted around and dove for his head, its gaping mouth flashing rows and rows of daggerlike teeth. He flinched, and the beast brushed past him so closely that he could feel the coolness of its scales.

He kept his eyes screwed shut, hoping against hope that what he had seen was his fevered imagination. But the persistent pain in his head and limbs kept dragging him back to reality. There was no denying what he knew to be true: he had let the *Enterprise* be boarded and taken over.

"Commander Riker," said an aristocratic voice, "I see you have rejoined us."

Riker felt himself moving, spinning around, and he opened his eyes to see that his bound body had been righted and was floating near the command chair. Yellow-garbed Elaysians manned most of the stations, although a few spindly Alpusta bounced around the circle of auxiliary consoles. The giant eel—he remembered it was called a Frill—cruised menacingly in front of the viewscreen, flapping long gossamer wings. It was like an alien menagerie had been set loose on his bridge.

Tangre Bertoran leaned over and gazed at him with a mixture of disgust, pity, and maybe even a little guilt. "I am truly sorry that you made us resort to these tactics."

"I'll bet," rasped Riker hoarsely.

"No, it's true. We are not pirates or brigands. We derive no pleasure from this. We don't fight wars—we have no weapons. That is why we must borrow yours."

"Where's my crew?" demanded Riker.

"They're all safe," answered the Elaysian. "No one was harmed. Once we turned off the gravity, it was quite easy to move everyone into your forward lounge while they were still unconscious. There are many advantages to low gravity."

"I wouldn't know," grumbled Riker. "I know there are no advantages to trying to help a bunch of ingrates like *you!*"

"Help us?" scoffed Bertoran. "You wanted to *doom* us. You would turn off the only protection we have against that *thing* out there . . . and wait until the last minute to do it! No thank you. We'll be happy to return your ship to you—*after* we destroy the rift."

Riker smiled, suddenly realizing why he was floating here in the middle of the bridge. "You can't get into the computer, can you? You can't target the weapons."

Bertoran sniffed disdainfully. "It's only a matter of time before we break your security codes. If need be, we can remove your weapons from their housings and mount them on the shell. Your technology doesn't hold any mysteries for us. However, it would be more efficient if you would cooperate with us."

"Duping me, knocking me out, and tying me up is *not* how you get my cooperation." Riker licked his dry lips. "I'll tell you what, if you release me and my crew right now and stop this unlawful hijacking, I won't report this to Starfleet."

The Elaysian gaped at him incredulously. "We are faced with *extinction,* and you threaten us with Starfleet? Commander Riker, you fail to realize how desperate we are. What is it—four days, and we'll all be dead? As far as Starfleet is concerned, we're *already* dead! You, me, this ship. . . . They're not sending any more rescue parties for us. They're closing our file."

Unfortunately, Riker couldn't argue that point. They had cheated death dozens of times, but this time death seemed to have a lot of allies.

"Well, if I'm dead," muttered Riker, "there isn't much you can do to me."

"Is that so?" asked Bertoran dryly. His gaze traveled from the bound human to the three-meter-long eel-shaped creature prowling in front of the viewscreen. As its filmy wings expanded and folded in slow rhythm, the beast cast a cold, fishy eye in Riker's direction. With a shudder, his eyes moved to the Frill's barracuda-like jaws and endless serrated teeth.

"In addition to our work on the shell," said Tangre Bertoran, "the Jeptah are also charged with providing ritual food to the Progeny, the Frills at the Blood Prism. I would think hard, Commander Riker, about how you wish you and your crew to end up—alive, or as part of a feeding frenzy."

Riker scowled and struggled mightily against his bindings. Floating in the air, unable to get any purchase with his feet, he just twisted around like a fish on a hook. The Frill cruised closer, obviously interested.

Time, thought Riker, *I've got to stall for time. Picard, Data, Deanna, Barclay, and Pazlar are still out there.*

"If it were up to me," rasped the human, "I'd tell you

to go to hell. But I can't make that decision for my whole crew. If they're all in one place, let me see them."

Bertoran frowned with concern. "I'm afraid I can't allow that. Our takeover of your ship was somewhat incomplete, due to your refusal to shut down your internal forcefields. You still have personnel at liberty in a few of your sensitive systems."

"I do?" croaked Riker, blinking his eyes with a ray of hope.

"I've taken steps to quash them," said Tangre Bertoran, his eyes narrowing.

Geordi La Forge and the rest of his engineering staff had barricaded themselves against the main doors of engineering, as armor-clad Alpusta tried to punch their way through with battering rams. Since the defenders were floating weightlessly and couldn't get any leverage, it was a futile tactic. They could easily grab heavy equipment to lay against the door, but every new blow sent the barricade and most of them reeling.

On the other side, the multilegged, multijointed Alpusta functioned perfectly well in the low gravity, since they could spread their legs to get purchase in every nook and cranny of the corridor. Even phaser beams glinted off their protective armor, and they worked in unison to rupture the door.

"More phasers!" shouted La Forge.

One of his engineers kept shooting into a jagged, protruding hole in the door, but it had no effect on the marauding Alpusta. "They've got armor or something!"

"Jeez!" muttered Geordi. "Let's get the hell out of here. Olswing, shoot a grappling hook at the Jefferies tube!"

It took a moment for the young ensign to realize exactly what La Forge wanted, but then he looked down at the crossbow in his hands, loaded with grappling hook and rope. The rope was intended to bolster the barricade, but now it had to serve another purpose. He gazed upward at engineering's high ceiling.

"Shoot it!" yelled La Forge, bracing himself to receive another smashing from the Alpusta.

Olswing took aim with the crossbow at the hatch of the Jefferies tube above his head and shot the self-puncturing grapple hook. It ruptured the ceiling near the hatch, expanded with a hiss of gas, and stuck. After tugging on the rope, the young ensign pulled himself hand-over-hand briskly through the low gravity and reached the ceiling in seconds. He quickly opened the hatch and scooted out of sight.

"Up the rope!" shouted Geordi, waving to his staff. "Everyone, up the rope!"

The techies virtually flew up the rope, swinging like monkeys in the low gravity. La Forge waited until the last member of his staff had fled, and with the main doors buckling, he hauled himself up the rope. With a tremendous crash, the Alpusta smashed the doors apart and surged into main engineering just as Geordi's legs disappeared into the Jefferies tube. The lead Alpusta shot a sticky web at his heels, but he slammed the hatch shut on the gooey filament.

"Climb! Climb!" yelled La Forge.

Hours flew by, but the exhilaration of soaring through the sparkling skies and towering prisms of Gemworld never lessened for Jean-Luc Picard. Because of the low gravity, a few well-timed bursts on his jet-pack kept him flying for kilometer after kilometer, zooming through the ever-shifting kaleidoscope of refracted light and multicolored clusters. He let Data and Keefe Nordine soar far ahead of him, always keeping their tiny silhouettes in sight amid the massive formations and endless blue sky.

It was so effortless, so free. He could understand why Nordine had let his limbs atrophy, and why Melora Pazlar had turned down a chance for surgeons to turn her into a conventional humanoid. *Once you have flown, it is hard to ever accept walking again.* For the first time, Picard felt he really understood why Gemworld had to be preserved, despite a nagging voice that told him there was a time to let dead worlds die.

Yes, it *was* an artificial world, but then so were most of the places where he spent his time. The manufactured environment of the *Enterprise* was nothing but a laboratory, and this was the laboratory of the Lipuls, Elaysians, Alpusta, Frills, Yilterns, and Gendlii. Was it so different? Life had to struggle for survival wherever it was, here or in the far reaches of space, or on some frozen moon. Maybe the inhabitants of Gemworld had become too complacent about their fragile world, thinking it would last forever. Maybe they forgot they still had to struggle. Hopefully they would be better prepared next time.

In the distance—it was hard to tell whether it was above them or below them—he could see a considerable number of small black dots. They had to be denizens of this world, but they were too distant for him to tell what species they were. So far in their journey, they had passed a few occupied clusters, including two Elaysian enclaves, but nobody had yet come out to meet them. However, this distant squadron of black dots appeared to be on an intercept course with them.

The captain tapped his combadge and shouted over the roar of the rushing wind. "Picard to Data!"

"Data here," came the reply.

"Do you see the flyers approaching us? To starboard!" That was as specific as he could get about direction.

"Yes, Captain. Should we move to intercept?"

"No, stay on course. Let's see if they're headed our way or it's just coincidence." He gave his jetpack a burst, accelerating toward the two figures ahead of him. "I'm closing the gap to bring us closer together."

"Acknowledged. Staying course to shuttlecraft."

A few seconds later, Picard zoomed past Keefe Nordine, and he pointed in Data's direction. Seconds after that, he pulled abreast of the android, and they shot through a gap between a rose prism and a lime-green one. He glanced back and saw Nordine pull within twenty meters. With monoliths on both sides of them, they had lost track of the other group of flyers, but he figured to catch sight of them when they exited.

Soaring from the cluster into open sky, Picard craned his neck to look for the larger group. He spotted them beneath his feet at five o'clock. They were so close, he could see the long strands trailing from their compact bodies. They weren't actually flying, but were swinging from crystal to crystal like trapeze artists.

His combadge chirped. "Data to Picard," said the android. "Those are Alpusta, and they clearly mean to intercept us."

"I agree," answered Picard. "Were they sent to find us?"

"Unknown. However, the Alpusta enclave is one of our destinations."

"Yes, I know." The captain frowned puzzledly as he soared through a crystalline archway sparkling in the sun. Unless he was totally turned around, the Alpusta enclave was in the opposite direction. These Alpusta could be coming from the shell, among other places. *Why so many of them? Fifty or sixty . . . just to deliver a message?*

Keefe Nordine zoomed up beside him, pointing back at their pursuers and shaking his head. "What gives?" he shouted.

"Let's halt!" Picard held up his hand, making sure Nordine got the message. Data was already doubling back, and the three of them formed a triangle in the shimmering sunlight.

The captain glanced back and saw the horde of Alpusta making their way jerkily yet inexorably toward their position. He didn't want to be unduly suspicious, but there was something ominous about this unruly advance across the sky. If someone had to relay a message, why didn't they use normal communications? His combadge was working.

Just to make sure, Picard tapped his badge. "Away Team One to *Enterprise.*" There was no answer, so he tapped it again. "Picard to *Enterprise.*"

"That is odd," said Data. "We are well within range." The android tried to contact the ship, with the same unsatisfactory result.

"Uh, gentlemen," said Keefe Nordine, edging closer to them. "I don't know much about Alpusta, but they don't look friendly. Did you do anything to upset them?"

Data cocked his head. "We were involved in an accident that killed five hundred of them."

"Is that right?" muttered the young man with another nervous glance. "And your ship doesn't answer. Just for the sake of argument, let's say we try to get to the other shuttlecraft as fast as we can. If they're friendly, it won't matter, will it?"

"Can we outrun them?" asked Picard.

"Unknown," answered Data, wrapping his hands around the controls of his jetpack. "There is only one foolproof way to find out."

The captain took another look at the approaching Alpusta, who fanned out across the sky. They looked like a sea of fat streamers bouncing off one prism after another, propelling dark warheads ever closer. He hadn't survived this long by ignoring the fine hairs on the back of his neck, and they were rising to attention. His inability to reach the *Enterprise* only fueled his anxiety.

"Should we alert Team Two?" asked Data.

"No, let them keep searching for the Lipuls' key," answered Picard. "It may be nothing." He stole another glance at the swarm of Alpusta bobbing ever closer on their retractable webs. As Nordine had said, they did not look friendly—and there were too many of them.

"Let's reach the shuttlecraft as soon as possible," he declared. "Same flying order as before, and don't get spread out."

"No problem there," said Nordine. "Let's fly!"

Data zoomed off toward a yellow cluster in the distance, and Nordine streaked after him. The captain twisted his hand controls, giving the jetpack a burst of fuel, and soared into the jutting, candy-colored landscape. But the thrill of flying was gone, replaced by the dread that something had gone wrong . . . terribly wrong.

Chapter Ten

GEORDI LA FORGE PANTED heavily and stared at the frightened engineers gathered around him in the storage closet off the stellar cartography room. He knew it was shielded by forcefields, thanks to the presence of hundreds of cosmic records on volatile magnetic media. In their spare time, the cartography staff had been transferring these records to newer media to preserve them.

Geordi wanted to make his way to one of the security lockers and get some more weapons, but that seemed pointless, since phasers hadn't done any good so far against the rampaging Alpusta. Luckily, the Alpusta were too large for the Jefferies tubes, so they had lost their pursuers for the moment.

He had no idea what had happened to the rest of the

crew, only that all his hails to the bridge or security had gone unanswered. He tried to think back to the chain of events. The last thing he remembered, the Jeptah on the shell were about to wrap them in their forcefields. Well, they had wrapped them in a lot more than that! They had put some kind of electroprotonic shock on the *Enterprise* that had knocked out all their systems and controls plus the artificial gravity. It must have knocked out most of the ship's personnel, too, and there was no way of telling if they were alive or dead.

Because of the shielding in engineering, he and his staff had been spared . . . for a while.

The chief engineer's jaw clenched with anger. The Jeptah had taken over the ship without firing a shot, and Geordi had personally given that pompous thug Tangre Bertoran all the information he'd needed to do it! He had wondered why they were so interested in the ship, although all of their questions had made sense at the time.

With his jaw set grimly, La Forge regarded the eight young engineers under his care: three humans, a Deltan, a Catullan, an Ardanan, and two small, blue-skinned Bynars. They were all floating in the cramped closet among a sea of small canisters and rolls of film, which were also floating. He batted a few canisters out of the way so that he could see everyone.

"I'm sorry I got you into this mess," he said. "I don't know how many others of the crew are still at liberty, but I'd be willing to bet it isn't very many."

He lifted his jaw with determination. "We have to proceed as if we're the only ones left and it's up to us to retake this ship."

That bold proclamation met with a lot of weary, frightened stares. *Right, we're going to retake this ship from hordes of nonhumanoids with nine poorly armed engineers.*

Geordi brushed another canister out of his face, cursing the lack of gravity. Then his expression brightened, his occluded eyes went wide, and he grabbed the small container from the air and kissed it.

"Sir, are you all right?" asked Olswing with concern.

"Yes!" answered La Forge with a big grin. "I know what will slow them down—grind them to a halt, in fact: Gravity! I've seen the Elaysians in gravity, and they're helpless. I imagine the Alpusta and all the rest of them are the same."

The young engineers looked at one another with fearful hope.

It still didn't sound like a very dangerous weapon, but Geordi knew it would be effective against this enemy. He rubbed his chin as he considered the problem. "All right, we know that they've stopped every system and then restored the ones they wanted, gravity not being one of them. There are hundreds of gravity generators embedded in the decks all over the ship. We know they didn't go around and tear them all up, so they're still there."

After a pause, he went on, "All they had to do was stop the graviton stream, probably by keeping the inertial damping fields off. Since the ship isn't moving, they don't need those either, but they're all tied in together. If we can get to the EPS power taps and overload them, the overload in the subspace field differential will be automatically bled off to the structural integrity field, which will kick the inertial damping fields back on—automatically! That should get the graviton stream moving again."

The two Bynars waved their hands excitedly. "There may be—" began one.

"A simpler way," ended the other. "We have hand-held graviton devices—"

"For the experiments we never got a chance to do. We can create—"

"Localized gravity fields."

"All right!" said Geordi with an evil smile. "Mobile weapons. I hate to ask, but where did we leave the graviton stuff for the experiment?"

"Cargo bay—"

"Sixteen." The Bynars smiled at each other with satisfaction.

"Once we leave here," said La Forge, "they can spot us with sensors, so we'll have to move fast. It may get difficult and dangerous. Are you with me?"

"Yes, sir! Let's go!" they shouted.

Geordi winked at his unlikely commandos. "We're going to have them crawling for mercy."

Deanna Troi slept uncommonly well floating under the struts of the shuttlecraft, even dressed in her environmental suit. A cool breeze carried by a warm convection current had washed away most of the globules of fouled marrow floating outside the icy prism, although she hadn't seen the cleansing action. Love could be cleansing, too, and she had done her best to unite two people who deserved a respite from the trials of Gemworld.

So she slept blissfully, content that she had done all she could. At first, her dreams made no sense: animals running in the forest, hunters pursuing them. Instead of being captured or killed, the frightened animals dashed off a cliff, plunging into a roiling purple sea. Disturbing as these images were, they weren't enough to wake her from her deep slumber, and she couldn't see how they related to her. It was like watching a holonovel featuring other people.

Finally she saw the ocean without the cliff and the frightened, suicidal animals. She could tell this was *her* ocean, the dream ocean she had inhabited ever since the first contact from the Lipuls. It was odd, she thought, how a dream can become more real than the reality it replaced, especially a dream that keeps recurring. She felt comfortable floating in this ocean, although not safe. . . . There was clearly no place that was safe.

In this dream, she remembered that she was looking for something—a crystal key. She could see the prize, hanging from a lanyard around the neck of a kindly man whose face filled the violet waters of her dream. His crystal key was also violet, and that seemed wrong somehow—wrong because it was not *her* crystal key, the one she was seeking.

It suddenly seemed as if this kindly white-haired man was evil, or had been taken over by evil. He had deep V-shaped ridges on his forehead, which marked him as the prey. Now Deanna was the hunter, stalking him, biding her time until she could get him alone and strike. If he lived, he would betray them. She didn't know why she was so certain of this, but it had to be true. Dreams don't lie.

So she waited until the victim was alone. In the ultimate betrayal, he had given up his violet crystal and didn't even possess it anymore. He was worse than the podlings who lived at the bottom of the mud and filth. She had a secret entrance into the programming room—the stream of gel behind the wall made especially for her, to give her access to the precious circuits.

She could see him through the misty crystal and quivering gel. When his hand reached for the small drawer and opened it, she smashed through the crystal and slammed onto his face, gripping tightly with her suction cups and tendrils. He thrashed about like a hunted animal who knew he was dying, but she held tightly, sucking the air from his lungs. Fragile creatures, these air-breathers.

In too short a time, his struggles were over, and he floated with his eyes wide open, not seeing. To escape, she swam through the air with difficulty, opening and closing like a miniature bellows. Fortunately, it was a short distance back to the slot in the wall. She closed the drawer behind her and slipped away into the stream of slow-moving liquid.

Now it was time to run, or *she* would become the hunted. The outsiders knew things, and the Hidden One knew *everything*. . . . They would chase her down.

At this point in the narration, the dreamer realized that she was quite mad. There could be no other explanation for taking another's life—such barbarism was simply not done except by the Frills. Distraught, grief-stricken, and feeling the weight of time, she gathered her crystal shard and brought it with her into the long, flowing stream. Her mind had been hopelessly corrupted, just as she had corrupted the fractal program.

Down, down she flowed—through the ancient streams and rivers, the ones that coursed no more on her beloved planet. Yet she could still feel the swift current, the ebbing of the tides. *I have lived too long. My world has lived too long. The Hidden One has come to collect the debt we never repaid.*

The dreamer shivered with this last realization. Maybe it could have all been avoided, but it was too late.

Weary and heartsick, she flowed into her ancestral home. But it had changed—the Hidden One was *here,* destroying, wreaking vengeance. She spirited the crystal shard into the drawer they had built to service the nourishment strand, thinking she would not defile the Holy Shard by dying with it. But die she must, before she betrayed her world any further.

And dream. She had to dream one more time, to make contact with the ones whom she had judged too hastily. *They* had frightened the Hidden One into action, not her, but their minds were so intertwined at this point that she had no defense against the darkness. She had lost her mind . . . or rather sacrificed it.

Deanna felt the warm tears squeeze from her eyes and cling to her eyelashes, unable to fall. She cried because she understood that they had arrived far too late to save the dreamer, or maybe even Gemworld itself. But now the subterfuge and denial were over, and the dreamer was going to accept the consequences.

Not waiting to die, the desperate creature sought out

the stifling black miasma; and she dreamed of the long-lost sea, as the blackness overtook her.

Still weeping, Troi shook herself awake and pulled her headgear off. After wiping the tears from her eyes, she swung herself up on the shuttlecraft and tapped her combadge.

"Troi to Barclay."

"Yes, sir?" came a sleepy voice.

"Open the hatch," she ordered. "I think I know where the Lipul left its key."

"Just a moment, sir." She heard thumping sounds in the small craft for a few seconds, then Reg opened the hatch. He had put back on his environmental suit, and Melora Pazlar was wearing her billowy native clothes.

"You received a dream?" asked Melora.

"More like a confession." Troi pulled herself into the cabin and pointed to the stasis canister. "I believe this dead Lipul is the one who sabotaged the shell and murdered Zuka Juno."

Melora looked shocked, then angry. "That's impossible."

"It's not impossible at all," answered Troi evenly. "It had access to the programming and the programming room when Zuka Juno was alone in there. It was on the shell when he died. I think Tangre Bertoran lied to us."

Melora licked her lips nervously, and Troi had a sudden insight. "You know he's been lying to us, don't you?"

Now it was Barclay's turn to look shocked. "C-Counselor Troi! Melora would never—"

"Can it, Reg. You don't know what's going on here. I don't even think the Elaysians know what's going on." Troi squinted her red eyes into the shimmering sunlight. "There's more to the dimensional rift than darkmatter and thoron radiation. There's an intelligence on the other side . . . with a very old score to settle. If I'm right about the shard, maybe I'm right about the rest of it."

She motioned to Pazlar. "Take us up to where the nourishment strand joins the crystal. There should be some kind of small access panel."

"Yes, ma'am." Melora looked dazed as she pulled herself into the pilot seat, as if her life and everything she believed in were spinning out of control.

Troi, on the other hand, felt more confident and relaxed than she had in days—since the first attack on her mind. She wasn't sure, but it seemed as if she could sense emotions again—at least she had read Pazlar's face like a computer screen. However, her mind was still not entirely her own, and she wasn't ready to claim victory.

Moments later they stopped the shuttlecraft at the weathered tip of the ice-blue prism, and Deanna was the first to fly out of the hatch. Melora caught up to her quickly, and together they reached the supply conduit where the strand joined the crystal. The nourishment tube was made from a biomass material that was part organic, part criss-crossed strands of wire, and the fittings gleamed like copper encrusted with turquoise. Deanna looked beneath the exotic fittings for the small drawer that allowed access for cleaning.

When she found it, she let out a yelp of joy, and she could see Melora staring intently at her. It was like the

Elaysian was watching a monster she had created as it came to frightful and unpredictable life.

"You know," said Troi, "you told the Lipuls to search me out, and they did. Now my mind is not my own."

Melora lowered her head. "I'm sorry."

Reg joined them, fidgeting nervously as he hovered behind her. She pointed to the access panel. "Do you want to open it?"

"G-Go ahead," breathed Barclay, clutching the crystal shards hanging from his neck.

The metal drawer was covered with ancient runes that Troi didn't know, but she knew she was destined to open it. She grabbed the ring handle and pulled the panel open with a scraping sound. Tumbling out came an exquisite crystal shard about twenty centimeters long and as clear as a diamond. It twirled in the air for several seconds before Troi snatched it by its white cord.

"Put it on," said Melora hoarsely. "You're the new proxy."

When Troi didn't act quickly enough, the Elaysian forcibly put the cord around her neck. Troi let go of the white crystal, and it floated like a feather in the warm breeze.

"We only need one more," said Reg.

Melora hung her head. "They'll never let you do it."

"What do you mean?" asked Troi.

Before Melora could answer, they heard a strange buzzing sound, like a thousand pairs of hummingbird wings. Melora spread her arms and caught enough wind to reach the tip of the blue prism, about twenty meters above the shuttlecraft. Eyes wide, the blond

Elaysian peered into the distance on the other side of the massive crystal.

"What is it?" asked Troi. Conscious of the precious artifact she wore around her neck, the Betazoid shoved off the weathered facet and drifted back to the shuttlecraft.

Melora just craned her neck upward, as the sky above her filled with a hundred Frills towing yellow-garbed Elaysians behind them. Their layered gossamer wings flapped in a tumultuous rhythm, creating a wind that blasted Deanna's hair back. The giant eel-like beasts strained at their reins as they pulled the Jeptah dignitaries into view.

One of the Elaysians waved to Melora. "Our daughter, you have done well! Tell the outsiders to surrender, and no harm will come to them."

"Surrender?" asked Reg indignantly. "I'm your acting senior engineer! Tell them, Melora!"

Deanna was now close enough to the shuttlecraft that she could duck in before any of those creatures could reach her, but Barclay was a problem. Melora was also too far away to be rescued, even if she wanted to be rescued; and that was not at all clear at the moment. One thing was certain—this was not a welcoming party.

"Melora!" yelled Reg, sounding like what he was—a wronged lover.

She turned to him tearfully. "I'm sorry, Reg!"

Troi used that moment of distraction to duck into the shuttlecraft and slam the hatch shut behind her. She had to ignore the look of horror on Barclay's face as he realized he had been abandoned, but she vaulted over the seats and reached the transporter in the rear of the craft.

With a glance out the window, she saw one of the Frills whip around like a snake, spread its wings, and shoot straight toward Reg. She homed in on his combadge, knowing she didn't have a second to lose, and she punched the panel to energize. With the monstrous jaws right on top of him, Reg threw up his arms to duck. Then he disappeared in a shimmering cloud of light as the beast swept through the sheen of his departed molecules.

Reg arrived on the transporter platform, floating and shivering in the air. Deanna grabbed the backs of the seats and vaulted into the pilot's seat. "I'm putting on gravity! Brace yourself."

Reg landed in a heap on the transporter platform and buried his face in his hands. "Melora!" he cried. "We've got to get her back!"

"Forget it, Reg, she's gone." This was literally true, because there was no sign of the Elaysian, the Jeptah, or their Frill mounts. They had all disappeared as rapidly as they had stormed over the top of the prism—although Troi assumed they were lurking on the other side of the massive blue crystal.

"Where did they go?" asked Reg.

Deanna shook her head. "Maybe they think we have weapons on the shuttlecraft. I'd take us out of here, but the captain is headed to meet us. We've got to warn him."

"That's probably how they found us," said Reg glumly. "The homing signal. I don't think it was *her* fault . . . she didn't betray us."

Troi turned back to look at the stoop-shouldered engineer with his hound-dog expression, and took pity on him. "Reg, I don't know what's going on, but I know that Melora knew something about this and didn't tell us. If she's sided with her own people—"

"She didn't!" insisted Reg irrationally. "I know she didn't."

Deanna simply shook her head, recalling how the Jeptah had thanked Melora by name. "If we contact the ship, maybe we can figure out what's going on."

"It must all be a misunderstanding," murmured Reg, toying nervously with his crystals.

Troi ignored his raw emotion for the moment to concentrate on her duty. "Away Team Two to *Enterprise*," she said, pressing the comm panel. When no one answered, she tried again. "Away Team Two to *Enterprise*. Troi to bridge. Come in!"

Now Barclay picked himself up from the deck and sat beside her, his red eyes really looking troubled. "That's weird."

"Yes, it is," agreed Troi. With determination, she pressed the combadge. "Troi to Picard."

"Picard here," came a breathless response, which was nearly drowned out by the sound of rushing wind.

"Captain, we found the Lipul's key, but something's gone wrong. A detachment of Jeptah tried to arrest us."

"And you can't reach the *Enterprise*."

"Right."

"We're being pursued by Alpusta," said the captain, "though I think we've lost them for the moment. Are you safe now?"

"No. I'm sure they're waiting nearby to see what we do. One more thing, Captain. We don't have our pilot anymore."

Beside her, Reg looked at her beseechingly, his hands held out, begging her to lie for Melora.

"She was captured," said Troi, feeling a knot in her stomach. "I don't feel comfortable flying the shuttle-craft around Gemworld—it's like a honeycomb."

"Just stay where you are, unless you have to move," ordered Picard. "We're still homing in on your signal. Once we make visual contact, we can try to lose them. Picard out."

Troi sat back in her seat and shivered. Although they were sitting in an enclosed ship in the middle of bright sunlight, she still felt a chill. It wasn't just for her, but for all those aboard the *Enterprise.* Had their hosts turned on them? For what purpose?

But Deanna knew there didn't need to be a purpose when people panicked. She also knew there were forces out there that none of them understood . . . and that none of them controlled.

"Thank you," breathed Reg beside her.

She knew he was thanking her for covering for Melora, but it also sounded like a thank-you for rescuing him—and just for being in command instead of him.

"Thank me when we get out of here," she answered.

"What are we supposed to do?"

"Wait." She gazed out the window at the perpetual sunlight, dappled with dancing glints of light refracted through the massive blue crystal. Gemworld appeared cheery and surreal as always, but that air of unreality didn't seem as charming as before.

There was something evil under the surface—growing, getting stronger, waiting to engulf them all.

Chapter Eleven

CARGO HOLD 16 WAS NOT as empty as Geordi La Forge would have liked, at least according to the tricorder readings he was getting. Teams of Alpusta were roaming the ship at will, moving with lightning speed for such big creatures, and were searching the cargo bays. He could only hope they wouldn't recognize what they found there.

No, thought Geordi, they had to be looking for weapons and survivors. His engineering staff had broken up into four teams, of two each; the other three teams were just supposed to keep moving in the Jefferies tubes, to confuse their pursuers. Only he and Olswing had the real mission: to liberate the portable graviton generators from the cargo bay. Without these weapons, they couldn't hope to reach the EPS power taps.

He and Olswing were two decks up in the Jefferies tube between decks 23 and 24, moving away from their destination. It wasn't healthy to stay in one place for more than a few seconds.

Wham! About twenty meters behind them, a blast of phaser fire punched into the Jefferies tube, gnawing an angry red hole in the bulkhead. The Alpusta had started to use their own phasers against them, shooting blindly at sensor blips in the tubes. La Forge and Olswing grabbed the handrails and propelled themselves along the rectangular tubes at breakneck speed, shooting like bullets in the weightless environment.

It was a good thing they were getting their quarry's positions sent to them from the bridge, thought Geordi, because they were always a few seconds behind. Although none of the survivors had been hit yet, Geordi didn't like his people being targets. They needed a safer, more effective diversion.

He motioned to Olswing to slow down, then he tapped his combadge. "Fox One to Fox Two."

"Fox Two here," answered the Deltan, who was paired with the Ardanan.

"Listen, are you still close to the forward torpedo room?"

"Close enough," answered the Deltan.

Somewhere behind them a phaser whined, and Geordi hurried himself along. "I want them to think we're attacking it—trying to destroy the torpedoes. That should draw off everyone on the lower levels. Tie your phaser to something and leave it on heavy stun, shooting into the torpedo room. Then get out of there— go back to the map room and wait for word."

"Yes, sir."

Geordi looked back at Olswing and whirled his finger in the air. At once they reversed direction and headed back down the way they had come. Pulling hand-over-hand, they were moving too fast in the low gravity to pay much attention to the scorch holes. The Alpusta were shooting at shadows, but they were still shooting.

When they again neared cargo bay 16, Geordi paused long enough to remove the tricorder from his belt. Still pulling himself along with one hand, he ran a quick scan of the large space below them. It was empty.

"It's time," he hissed to Olswing. The engineer stowed the tricorder and picked up speed, flying fearlessly straight down. He stuck his hands out in front of him and burst through the hatch into the high-ceilinged, nearly empty cargo hold.

There were a few colorful storage barrels and large metal boxes floating about. Geordi tucked into a ball and bounced off the deck, making straight for one of the galvanized boxes. Behind him, Olswing did the same, and they caught the boxes and glided to the ceiling.

Without warning, the main doors whooshed open, and a long-legged Alpusta leaped into the room. Geordi fumbled with the latch on the box, trying to get it open, but he could see the Alpusta awkwardy handling a phaser rifle. With no time to spare, he pushed off the ceiling and ducked behind one of the floating barrels.

The Alpusta got off a hurried shot, but he was no marksman; the beam streaked past Geordi, raking the bulkhead in a sizzling glow. Olswing got his box open, and he pulled out a cylindrical graviton discharger. It didn't look like a weapon, on its ungainly tripod, and he worked feverishly to unfold it.

The spidery Alpusta bounded into the cargo hold, tossing away the unfamiliar phaser rifle. Instead it shot an extension rod that speared Olswing in the thigh. He screamed with terror and dropped the graviton device. The Alpusta chittered with excitement and slowly retracted its web, reeling Olswing in like a harpooned fish.

Behind the floating barrel, Geordi finally pried his box open and pulled out a wide-beam graviton disperser. There was no reason to even aim this box-like device; activating it would be enough.

Olswing screamed and flailed his arms as the monstrous beast pulled him toward its armored torso. Geordi flicked a switch, noticed the blinking lights come on, and tossed the machine in the Alpusta's direction.

As soon as the box got within about six meters, the Alpusta deflated like a punctured balloon. It spun around several times and collapsed in a pathetic ball on the deck. Olswing landed in a heap on top of the creature, squishing it within its suddenly oppressive armor. He got momentarily entangled in its flailing legs, but he managed to scramble away.

La Forge moved quickly to grab the other device, the graviton discharger, and snagged the cylinder just as another Alpusta bobbed into the entrance. Geordi didn't hesitate to aim the gravity device and activate it. At once the Alpusta's legs went as stiff as curtain rods, and it shuddered as if speared on an invisible lance.

Geordi motioned to Olswing, who was in obvious

pain, gripping his bloody thigh. "Get the disperser and get out! Through the Jefferies tube!"

With a grimace, the ensign pushed off from the deck and drifted to the hatch, grabbing the floating box on the way. La Forge scanned the cargo bay, wishing they could take more equipment, but he could already see cautious shadows gathering in the corridor. Geordi retreated, keeping the graviton beam trained on the poleaxed Alpusta in the entrance.

Clutching his new weapon to his chest, Geordi shot up the hatch and was gone. This was the last time he planned to run from these suckers, because now they had the means to go on the attack.

On the bridge of the hijacked ship, Will Riker twisted in his bindings, but he still couldn't get any traction in the low gravity. For what seemed like hours now, they had let him dangle in the breeze while they went about the twin tasks of breaking the computer control over the weapons systems and finding the scattered remnants of his crew.

He couldn't tell how either task was going, but there had been a flurry of activity a few minutes ago. It had seemed like an agitated flurry, and Tangre Bertoran had stormed off with the Frill and several Alpusta in tow. Other yellow-garbed Elaysians and Alpusta kept working at the bridge stations. These code-breakers were meticulous and intent on their task, and Riker feared they would eventually be successful.

He was fearful because they had given up trying to make him talk. In fact, they had all but forgotten about him.

Riker twisted and struggled anew against his tight bonds, but he only succeeded in rubbing more skin off his wrists and ankles. He was helpless, and the majority of his crew were also helpless. He had no idea what had happened to the two away teams, except that the captain had lost his shuttlecraft. Riker could only presume that they had been caught by surprise, as he had been. Maybe they'd resisted, like the few survivors on the ship. At this point, he could only hope.

Soaring through the jutting crystal canyons of Gemworld, Captain Picard found it hard to believe this fantasy land had turned against them. He glanced behind him and saw no sign of their pursuers or of any other living thing. It was as if they had fallen off the edge of civilization into a primeval world, and then had just kept falling.

He could barely feel his legs, they were so numb from hours of being whipped by the wind as they hung from the jetpack. Picard could sympathize with the flyer ahead of him, Keefe Nordine, who had lost much of the muscle mass in his legs from his prolonged stay on Gemworld. Nordine wasn't getting any better doing this, and Picard vowed to himself that he would make it up to the young civilian.

The captain tried to put his worry over his ship out of his mind. Until they had some answers, he couldn't formulate a plan—or even a theory—about what had happened. The away teams were in survival mode, dependent upon each other, and the *Enterprise* would have to fend for herself. He hated being so cavalier about it, but circumstances didn't leave him much choice. Until they had reason to alter their plans, they had to stay on mission and collect the six crystal keys.

They were so close, with five keys already in hand. On the face of it their mission had been successful, but it certainly didn't feel that way. Losing contact with the *Enterprise,* being chased halfway across the sky—these weren't developments he had anticipated.

His combadge beeped. It was Data's wind-battered voice. "Captain, we are almost there. However—"

The android didn't need to finish, because the captain saw them—a huge flock of dark shapes sweeping over the top of an ice-blue crystal, heading to intercept them. It was almost a relief to see other living creatures after their long journey, even if the creatures were inexplicably hostile.

"I see them," he answered. "Take evasive action until we contact the shuttlecraft. Make sure Nordine follows you."

"Yes, sir."

Picard tapped his combadge again. "Picard to Troi."

"Troi here."

"We're almost at your position—your friends are coming to greet us."

"I see them moving," answered Troi. "We'll follow them to you. Barclay says we can make a smoke cloud by venting the cryo tanks and the vectored exhaust at the same time."

Picard smiled in spite of the danger. "It says in the manual not to do that, but I won't report you. Picard out."

He worked the hand controls, noting that his fuel was down to one-eighth of a tank. He would exhaust a lot of that right now as he shot several hundred meters straight up, chasing Nordine and Data, who were already zooming up and over the approaching horde.

They looked beautiful and deadly, the sinewy Frills with their quivering, radiant wings. The haughty Jeptah who flew in their wake, clutching their golden reins, were of little consequence; Picard could only think of those massive jaws and gleaming teeth. The Frills were more than transportation—they were a weapon.

There had to be a hundred of them, swooping upward to catch the three lone flyers. Data led them between a stark green prism and a curved lavender archway, forcing the Frills and Elaysians into a narrow stream of about ten riders across. Despite cranking his controls to full acceleration, Picard could feel the sleek predators gaining on him. They moved much faster than the Alpusta, and he knew they would get caught if the chase lasted too long.

He heard a roar, and he glanced over his shoulder in time to see the shuttlecraft go slicing through the flock of Frills and Jeptah. Maybe Troi wasn't confident of her flying, but she was doing all right—she sent at least a dozen of them scattering. But the others regrouped and came tearing after them, their wings beating the air in unison, causing an ominous hum.

That was when Troi cut loose with a billowing white cloud of ice crystals and exhaust fumes that engulfed the lead Frills and obscured everything behind them. Seeing this, Data stopped his breakneck ascent and came banking around in a broad loop. Nordine and Picard did likewise, and the shuttlecraft blew by them so close that Picard could feel the heat of its thrusters.

Troi shot several hundred meters past them before she realized that she had to stop. She fired reverse thrusters, and the shuttlecraft spun to a stop. The small craft floated ahead of them like an island of sanity in a world gone mad. The three flyers lost no time in aiming their frail bodies at the craft and gunning their jets.

The smoke had caused considerable chaos behind them, but the Frills were fearless and kept coming. Scores of them broke through the smoke and soared after the outsiders, their jaws snapping with agitation.

Data was the first to reach the shuttlecraft, and there was no time for niceties such as opening the hatch. The android grabbed a strut and hung on with one arm while he turned and waved his free hand in the air. He virtually snagged Nordine out of the sky as he flew past.

Picard could hear beating wings bearing down on him, and he reached the shuttlecraft just as ferocious jaws clamped shut on his jetpack. He was tossed like a rag doll in a dog's mouth, and he felt a whip strike him on the face as a Jeptah lashed out with his reins. More Frills headed toward him, their eyes and jaws wide with frenzy.

Suddenly a red phaser beam ripped into the Frill, searing off its head and spewing a mist of green blood into the air. Freed from the ferocious jaws, Picard managed to right himself and get another thrust from his jets; he hurtled toward the shuttlecraft.

As Nordine scrambled out of the way, Data let go of his phaser and lowered his hand beneath the strut. He snagged Picard as he went rushing past, and the android held him with his incredible strength until the captain could cut his jets. The Frills bore down on them, and the sky seemed filled with jagged teeth and whirring wings.

As the three flyers clung to the struts for their very lives, Troi fired her thrusters, and the shuttlecraft spun around and pulled away. The angry swarm kept after them, with the Jeptah urging the Frills onward, but they were no match in speed for the shuttlecraft. Gradually they began to increase their lead and pull away into the sparkling blue sky.

Troi piloted them around the base of a large red cluster, trying to give them some cover. As soon as she came to a stop, the hatch popped open and Barclay stuck his hand out to pull them in. The captain had never been so glad to see a helping hand and he threw himself into the cabin.

"Hurry! They're coming back!" shouted Barclay.

Data did a graceful flip like a gymnast, landing perfectly in the doorway. He yanked Nordine into the craft just as a Frill shot past, barely missing his legs with its gaping jaws. It was crowded and chaotic inside the shuttlecraft, as the flyers suddenly had to deal with the sensation of gravity while still wearing their jetpacks, but Picard managed to stumble to the rear of the craft and collapse. He dragged Nordine after him, while Data slammed the hatch shut in the teeth of a diving Frill.

Thuds sounded all around them as the Frills attacked the hull, but Troi put on the shields, resulting in screams and sizzling sounds. Picard turned away from the chaos outside the hull as Data jumped into the pilot's seat.

"Still taking evasive maneuvers," said the android calmly. Under his skilled hands, the shuttlecraft was soon soaring between candy-colored prisms, having left their pursuers far behind.

The captain finally let out his pent-up breath and slid out of his jetpack. He inspected the impressive teeth marks on the fuel tank, glad that it wasn't the skin on his back.

"Captain, what is our course?" asked Data.

Picard took a thoughtful breath and rubbed his tingling legs. "How far are we from the *Enterprise?*"

"It would take approximately eight hours to reach the *Enterprise.*"

The captain nodded solemnly. "And to the Alpusta enclave?"

"Six-and-a-half hours," answered Data. "That is very approximate."

Captain Picard scowled, not liking any of his options. "We're so close to having all six crystals that I don't want to stop now, but we've got to get some answers."

"Data," cut in Deanna, "how far are we from the Gendlii?"

After consulting his instruments, the android replied, "Approximately two hours and fifteen minutes."

"I don't know why we should go there," said Troi, shaking her head, "except that it's close and we might get some answers."

"There's an old saying," said Captain Picard, managing a weary smile. " 'Any port in a storm.' Set course for the Gendlii, and keep trying to raise the *Enterprise* and the shell."

"Yes, sir."

The captain heard Data's efficient voice speaking into the communications channels; the android could keep that up for hours, as he tried to contact the *Enterprise*. Picard let out a long sigh and looked around at the expectant faces: Troi, Barclay, and Keefe Nordine.

"So how did we lose Pazlar?" he asked.

Reg started to stammer an answer, but Deanna touched his shoulder to shut him up. "We had just recovered the Lipuls' crystal key." Self-consciously she stroked the clear shard now hanging from her neck.

"Good work," cut in Picard.

"I'll tell you about that in a second." Troi shot another glance at Barclay, who wrung his hands nervously. "Anyway, we were too close to the monolith to see them coming, and they took us by surprise. They demanded that we surrender, without an explanation. Melora was closer to them, and she tried to reason with them. When that didn't work, they tried to capture us. I managed to get into the shuttlecraft and transport Barclay, but they flew off, taking Melora with them."

Barclay nodded several times. "Yes, that's how it happened . . . d-definitely."

Picard scratched his chin, thinking that he had not gotten the whole story but that it was enough for now. "You started to say, Counselor, about how you found the Lipuls' key even though the senior engineer was dead."

"Yes, sir."

The captain listened in rapt attention and even Data leaned closer, as Troi told them about her remarkable dream. In addition to learning the exact location of the shard, she concluded that the Lipul senior engineer had been the one who had sabotaged the shell and murdered its Elaysian counterpart, Zuka Juno. It was a shocking revelation, although it fit the facts. The image of the Lipul shooting through an access panel and smothering the helpless Elaysian was troubling, and Picard couldn't help but ask, "Why?"

"Because of something that's out there in that rift," Troi answered gravely. "This has come to me in bits and pieces—some of it from the Gendlii—but I'm certain that the Lipuls have traveled to that dimension in their dreamships. That was long ago, before the rift opened. I don't know exactly what they found in that dimension, but there was a plethora of life . . . and an overriding intelligence. . . . An entity. . . . I believe the Lipuls stole something from that other dimension, and that the entity learned to travel as they travel."

Deanna pointed out the window. "I believe that entity opened the rift. It must have corrupted the Lipul senior engineer and forced it to perform these acts. I know that it can get inside your mind."

The captain nodded solemnly and met her eyes. "Was this thing inside your mind when you were delirious?"

"Yes," she answered hoarsely. "And I don't know how much control I'll have if it comes back. Maybe it's there now, for all I know."

"What about the Elaysians and the other species?" asked Picard. "Has this thing affected them?"

Troi shook her head. "My gut instinct is that they're just scared—panicked. I don't think they ever intended to let us shut down their shell. The Jeptah have resented us calling the shots from the beginning, so they're probably trying to take over. If you think about it, only the Lipuls sent for us—they're the only ones who knew how bad it was."

The captain stood up and stretched his wobbly legs. "Any luck hailing them, Mr. Data?"

"No, sir, no one responds."

"Mr. Nordine, you're the only local expert we have now," said the captain. "Do you have an opinion on any of this?"

"Maybe," said the young man. "I was thinking that if *all* the Alpusta, Elaysians, and Frills were after us, we would never have gotten away. The skies would be full of them as far as you could see. I think it's just a small batch that are causing trouble for you. I know about the Jeptah—they wield a lot of power, but there aren't very many of them, numerically."

"That's my conclusion, too," said Captain Picard resolutely. "Mr. Data, keep the shields up and proceed to the Gendlii enclave."

"Yes, sir."

The captain remained stoic, but inside his stomach was churning. He was operating on a lot of conjecture and very little information, most of it divined from dreams and dreamlike encounters with bizarre creatures. Now they were looking to a gigantic fungus for answers.

Despite their lack of information, the silence from his ship spoke volumes.

Melora Pazlar shivered after her molecules reassembled and she found herself floating in a familiar place, a transporter room aboard the *Enterprise*. Hovering before her was Tangre Bertoran and a retinue that included two Jeptah, a large Frill, and a fully armored Alpusta. She had not seen an Alpusta wearing armor since she was a child, in a holiday parade, and it was frightening to see it here and to realize that it wasn't for show.

"I thought it wasn't safe to transport long distances," she told Bertoran as she pushed herself off the transporter platform.

He smiled condescendingly. "You may notice that we no longer take orders and advice from the outsiders. Now we control the situation—and all the technology."

Melora held her tongue and didn't call him a backstabbing liar. He had never told her he was planning to take over the *Enterprise*. She would never have agreed to that. Too late, she realized that she had let her loyalty to her people blind her, that she had backed the wrong side—the unscrupulous side.

All Melora said was, "If you're in charge, why do you need *me?* I thought I could go back to my enclave and wait for the end, whatever it is."

Bertoran grimaced, as if he had been unpleasantly inconvenienced. "Although we are in charge here, as you can see, we have some unfinished business. There are a handful of Starfleet crewmembers still at liberty on the ship causing problems. We thought you could make an announcement to them—talk some sense into them."

Melora had to laugh. "You want me to try to convince a Starfleet crew to surrender their ship? You haven't learned very much about them. They're loyal and tenacious—they don't give up, unlike me."

Now the Peer of the Jeptah scowled. "You won't help us?"

"Why do you need this ship, anyway?" asked Melora, trying to stall for time while she figured out what to do.

"To use their weapons on the rift, of course," answered Bertoran.

Melora hoped that her face didn't betray her horror. Starfleet weapons were not experimental toys to be shot off like fireworks. She had been in the meetings when the captain and his staff had discussed using weapons on the rift, but they knew nothing about it. The Jeptah also knew nothing about it. The only ones who knew anything were the Lipuls—and maybe their chosen, Deanna Troi.

"You have no idea what effect those weapons will have," she burst out, forgetting her studied neutrality. "And you don't know what's on the other side. There's another dimension out there . . . life-forms you know nothing about!"

"We know the rift is destroying Gemworld, and now we have the means to destroy *it*." Tangre Bertoran folded his arms and looked crossly at her. "I'm going to give you another chance to prove your loyalty to your homeworld. For reasons that are too long to go into, we have removed one of the phaser banks from the ship and have mounted it on the shell. That's fourteen phaser emitters. We can figure out the technology, but you're familiar with Starfleet nomenclature—you could cut our preparation time considerably."

"All right," said Melora, unable to think of anything else to say. It was best to stay at liberty herself than to be imprisoned by these arrogant fools.

"We plan to fire the phasers in one shadow mark," declared Bertoran, his blue eyes narrowing. "So you, my compatriots, and I will transport over to the shell and begin final preparations."

As the big Alpusta and the sleek Frill moved forward, Melora felt herself crowded back onto the transporter platform. They weren't taking any chances—they certainly weren't going to leave her alone with their new toy. If she was going to redeem herself, she would have less than an hour to do so.

Chapter Twelve

"LET IT RIP!" ordered Geordi La Forge.

The two diminutive Bynars shot forward with the disperser and flooded the corridor with gravitons. At once the two Alpusta in the corridor constricted like spiders that had been stabbed with a hot poker, and an Elaysian crashed into the bulkhead. Nevertheless, the Elaysian managed to keep his wits about him, and was fumbling in his yellow robes for a phaser when the Catullan let loose with the graviton discharger from the other end of the corridor. The loop formed a gravity field, and the horrified Elaysian went crashing to the deck. He could barely lift his arm, and a Bynar ran forward, leaped over a fallen Alpusta, and kicked the weapon out of his hand.

Three more engineers poured into the corridor, running and jumping like hurdlers over the twitching legs of the Alpusta. One of the humans kicked an armored Alpusta and sent it flying, but he yelped in pain and tumbled to the deck, gripping his toe.

"Just get to the power taps!" shouted La Forge angrily. Hanging from the Jefferies tube in the ceiling, he spotted movement behind the Catullan. "Pakoch, behind you!"

The Catullan whirled around with the graviton discharger, which cut the field in the corridor. He caught another Alpusta by surprise, and the gangly creature was poleaxed and spun around, its legs clattering against the walls of the corridor. The Bynars scrambled to readjust the graviton disperser, and they were able to establish a new field for their comrades, who were uncapping the power taps. The Deltan waited behind them with a disassembled phaser that would overload the power system and bleed off to the structural integrity field. That would kick on the inertial damping field and the artificial gravity.

The Jeptah thought *they* were obsessive about redundant systems, mused Geordi, but they had nothing on Starfleet ship designers.

"Hurry!" he shouted, hearing voices coming from the turbolift. "Reinforcements are on the way."

"Almost there!" shouted the Deltan.

The humans fell back from the open access panels, and the Deltan skillfully plugged in the phaser's power supply. Now all they had to do was defend this corridor until the chain reactions started, and that was the job of their two little machines.

"Widen the field!" shouted the chief engineer.

Again the Bynars repositioned the portable devices, checking the results on a tricorder. All of this seemed to be taking forever, and he could hear Alpusta flying down the corridor.

"Hit the deck!" he shouted.

His squadron of unlikely commandos threw themselves to the deck as a horde of clattering, chittering Alpusta shot into the area. When they hit the gravity, they went spinning out of control like hairy black pinwheels, crashing and careening off the bulkheads. His people had to roll and scramble to keep from getting impaled by the flying legs and webs. When it was all over, gravity had wreaked a terrible toll, with at least six crumpled Alpusta and two Elaysians lying very still.

Then Geordi felt himself falling out of the Jefferies tube, and he just barely hung onto the rungs, his feet dangling beneath him with the sudden gravity.

Will Riker dropped like a bag of bricks to the deck, his fall broken somewhat by the command chair. He bounced off its arm and rolled on top of an Elaysian. The startled humanoid stared at him as if she had no idea why she was suddenly impaled upon the deck by an invisible force.

He smiled at her and said, "It looks like you've come down to my level."

Riker rolled off her and turned around to see what else was happening. All over the bridge, Elaysians and Alpusta lay crumpled on the deck, looking like discarded toys. Many of them managed to move and pull themselves up onto elbows and leg joints, but they looked crushed and stunned. One Alpusta thrashed about as if it wanted to fight its invisible opponent but didn't know where it was.

A minute later, the turbolift doors opened, and La Forge and several of his engineering staff charged onto the bridge. One of the Alpusta shot a web at Geordi that fell far short, and Geordi shot it with a phaser rifle. Although his shot didn't have much effect, it caused most of the Alpusta to shrink away, the fight seeping out of them.

La Forge grabbed one of the Elaysians and stuck the phaser rifle to his head. In no uncertain terms, he said, "Surrender."

The Elaysian nodded his head. "Yes! Yes!"

Two Bynars rushed toward Riker, pulling identical blades from their utility belts. In a few slashes, they hacked his bindings away, and he moved his aching limbs.

"Thank you! Good job," he breathed.

"Do you require—"

"Medical assistance?" they asked.

Will groaned and rubbed a stiff shoulder. "I'm all right. Good job, Geordi!"

"Thanks," answered the engineer with a grin. "Now I'd like to find Tangre Bertoran and drop him on his head."

"Me, too." Riker rolled over and staggered to his feet. He braced himself on the command chair and tapped his combadge. "This is Commander Riker to all hands. Our engineering staff has retaken the ship. All invading forces, lay down your weapons and cease to resist, or you will be dealt with in the harshest manner."

About ten meters away from him, an Elaysian slid a hand phaser across the deck, and it clattered to a stop in front of Riker. The Jeptah dropped his head onto the cold surface, as if he didn't have the strength to lift it.

Riker strode over, lifted the man up, and dragged him to the ops station, tossing him into the seat. "Get your boss—I want to talk to him."

Melora Pazlar gazed out the observation window at the large phaser array mounted on the shell, aimed at the void of space. The blackness, with its light sprinkling of stars, looked oddly peaceful compared to the chaos that had become Gemworld. She once had a life out there among the stars, but that life had been irreparably dashed to bits by her own stupidity. Now it appeared that the only other life she had ever known was about to die a miserable death, due to the stupidity of others.

Worse yet, innocent people—and a good man who loved her—were going to suffer because of her. Maybe she couldn't have prevented Bertoran's deception, but she could have tried harder. She was supposed to be the liaison between their two worlds—that's why the Lipuls had chosen her—but she had failed in all her duties.

"Daughter!" called Tangre Bertoran from the monitoring station behind her. "Narrow beams are created by rapid segment-order firing, aren't they?"

Melora sighed and answered, "Yes. A wider beam, or cone beam, results from slower firing rates."

Bertoran nodded and consulted with his retinue of two Elaysians and an Alpusta. Their animated voices carried across the cylindrical chamber, but Melora scarcely paid them any attention. So far, she had given them accurate answers, because she was too weary and disheartened to lie anymore. The Frill shook its wings and drifted lazily through the long chamber, casting a cold, suspicious eye at her.

She turned back to the odd sight outside the window on the pitted surface of the shell. Melora had seen phaser banks before, when she had done emergency spacewalks during the war, but she had never seen one ripped from a ship's hull and mounted on the stalks of what used to be hydrogen collectors. It seemed just one more benign system that had been corrupted for the cause of evil.

Suddenly the door at the end of the chamber opened, and a worried-looking Jeptah fluttered into the room. "Master?"

Tangre Bertoran glared at him. "I thought I left orders not to be disturbed. Now get out of here!"

"Master, this is urgent," insisted the distraught Jeptah. "Word received from the *Enterprise*—the Starfleet crew has recaptured the ship!"

"What?" roared Bertoran. "Impossible!"

"No, sir, not impossible," said the messenger with a frightened gulp. "The renegades managed to restore the synthetic gravity. Commander Riker wishes to speak to you."

Tangre Bertoran looked stricken with fear for a moment, then smiled. "Give them another protonic pulse."

The underling looked horrified. "But, sir, we have fifty people over there. They've put up their shields—it won't be effective."

"It will delay them!" shouted Bertoran. "We're almost ready here. A few more tweaks on the prefire segments and we'll have just the pattern and trajectory we need."

Melora whirled around, unable to hide her disgust. "Don't you care that you stole their ship, stole their weapons, and used their good will against them? You've treated them like podlings. They're within their rights to kill us all!"

"They won't fire on the shell," said Bertoran confidently. "Even if they do, our forcefields will hold long enough."

"I'm not helping you anymore," declared Melora.

"I never trusted you anyway." Bertoran motioned to the Alpusta at his side, and the gangly creature shot a thick web at Melora. She was too surprised to react quickly enough, and the sticky strand wrapped around her arms and gripped her tightly. She struggled for a few seconds, but she wasn't going to move more than a few centimeters.

"Don't worry, Daughter," said the Peer of the Jeptah, sounding once more like a kindly professor, "we will always consider you a hero, because you did bring us the means of our salvation. In a few minutes, the rift will be destroyed, and we can be friends with the Federation again. All will be forgiven and forgotten."

"No," said Melora tearfully. "Even if it works, all will not be forgiven!"

Bertoran turned to the messenger by the door. "You have your orders. Go!"

"Yes, Master." The Jeptah bowed and hurried out the door with a flutter.

Melora struggled against the sticky bindings, but she knew it was no use. It wasn't Bertoran who would never be forgiven—it was *she*. She would never forgive herself for what she had done to her shipmates . . . and Reg. The young lieutenant lowered her head and wept quietly for the death of her planet . . . and of her love and innocence.

On the bridge, Riker staggered as the ship was jolted. "What was that?" he growled.

"The same kind of protonic shockwave that hit us before," answered La Forge on the ops station. "Our shields are holding. No damage."

Will gritted his teeth and strode to the tactical station, taking over the unmanned console himself. They had locked up almost a dozen prisoners in the captain's ready room, and he hoped they weren't destroying the place.

"I think we'll give them a little bit of their own medicine," vowed Riker.

"Be careful," warned Geordi. "Our repair crews are just reporting in . . . and things are missing."

"What things?"

Geordi looked back at him with a worried expression. "Like a full phaser bank from the aft saucer array."

"Damn Bertoran!" grumbled Will, slamming his fist into his palm. "He said he would steal the weapons if he couldn't break the codes."

"At least he kept his word about that," said La Forge.

The turbolift doors opened, and three more crewmembers rushed onto the bridge. "A repair crew finally

193

unsealed the lounge," reported one of them. "All the crew is accounted for."

"That's good news," said Riker. "Go ahead and take your posts. We've got to get out of here."

"Slowly," warned Geordi. "We've got a hull breach where they ripped out that phaser bank."

"All those phaser emitters," muttered Riker worriedly as he stared at the implacable shell on the viewscreen. "With their power sources, they can do a lot of damage."

"What is their target?" asked La Forge, turning to look at his old friend. "It's not us, is it?"

Riker scowled and shook his head. "No. They've got bigger fish to fry."

On the shuttlecraft, Deanna Troi had just settled back in her seat and closed her eyes, hoping to take a short nap before they reached the Gendlii. She might need her strength and her wits about her.

Before sleep could wrap her in blissful ignorance, the comm board crackled with such noise that it made everyone jump. A familiar voice boomed from the panel, and it sounded tense and angry. *"Enterprise* to all away teams."

"Data here. We are now combined into one away team," answered the android. "It is good to hear your voice, Commander. We were unable to reach you."

"I know." Everyone on the shuttle leaned forward to hear his explanation. "Tangre Bertoran pulled a fast one on us and managed to take over the ship for several hours. We're in control now, but the situation is still tenuous. The biggest problem is that they're in control of one of our phaser banks. They physically moved it to the shell."

"Blast it," muttered the captain. "Picard here. What steps have you taken to neutralize them?"

"We're just digging out from under, Captain. I learned about this a moment ago. We're moving at slow speed with a hull breach just to get away from them. I'm hesitant to use weapons on the shell, because we really don't want to lose all the atmosphere."

"Have you seen Lieutenant Pazlar?" broke in Reg Barclay, loudly and worriedly.

"Pazlar? No. I thought she was with you."

The captain scowled. "What about boarding parties? Can you send anyone over to the shell?"

"It's a huge place, and we don't know where they are. We would have to destroy their forcefields just to—"

Deanna intended to keep listening, but communications suddenly went dead. Or at least it went dead in her mind, replaced by a frightening rumble that grew into a primal scream. It was so awful that she covered her ears and bent over, her torso twisting between her knees. But she kept her eyes open—which was a terrible mistake, because the deck beneath her feet was ripping apart, revealing a pool of blackness. She screamed and tried to leap upward to escape from the rift yawning beneath her feet, but demonic hands grabbed her. There was a babble of voices in her head, and she fought them off with her own incessant babble.

"I won't go! I can't! Get away from me!" she screamed.

The pool of blackness beneath her feet rose up and ripped the deck open like it was cheap tin. Then the blackness began to spin like a whirlpool of darkmatter, sucking her in by her legs.

Deanna screamed in stark terror, trying to grab the roots that were the only thing saving her from the dark abyss. The blackness wanted her and was determined to swallow her whole—it was angry and hurt, lashing out at everything on their plane of existence. She wanted to fight, but it was no use—the dark pool consumed her like the gaping jaws of a giant Frill.

"Look out!" shouted Reg Barclay. He ducked, but he needn't have feared, because Data saw the huge red monolith shaking like a twig in front of them. He turned hard to port as a crystal finger broke off, spinning slowly like a demented windmill, swerving into their path. Gemworld was falling apart!

Reg stared down at Deanna Troi, who was comatose in the captain's arms. He almost wished it were him.

Chapter Thirteen

MELORA DIDN'T REALIZE anything was wrong until she heard Tangre Bertoran shout in alarm. She shook herself out of her lethargy and looked up—she could hear the window shaking in its frame, and the aged metal was groaning. The shell was falling apart!

She knew they had fired the phasers, but she refused to watch until now. "You idiot!" she shouted at Bertoran. "Turn it off!"

He was staring intently at his readouts, but the Alpusta and the Frill were in full panic, in a race to get to the door. With the Alpusta letting go of its web, Melora found that she could twist out of the sticky strands. She didn't think; she just reacted with all the pent-up anger inside her. With muscles built up from ten years of fighting gravity, she pushed off the wall and streaked across the chamber. She plowed hard with both fore-arms into Bertoran's back, sending him careening head first into an unforgiving bulkhead. His head split open like a melon.

With the shell shuddering all around them, engineers from three species stared as Bertoran's white hair turned as dark as the mutant crystal. He mouthed some-thing, but the light was already fading from his eyes. Melora reached him first and tried to shake some life back into him, but his body hung like an empty space-suit in her hands.

"I'm shutting off the phasers!" shouted another Jep-tah, flying to the board and pounding in some com-mands. A moment later, the awful groaning and shuddering stopped, but it wasn't soon enough to save Tangre Bertoran. Melora let go of the limp body and stared wild-eyed at him, her blond hair standing on end.

"You killed him!" said a second Elaysian in aston-ishment. The Frill and the Alpusta stopped moving and regarded her warily, recognizing death as the ultimate arbitrator.

"I didn't mean to," she breathed. "I was only trying to stop him. Did you feel the shell trembling?"

No one answered. The others shrank back from her in fear. "It was *destroying* us!" she shouted. "Tangre Bertoran was destroying us. Look at your instru-ments—is the darkmatter still bombarding us? Is the thoron radiation still at deadly levels? Look!"

The two Elaysians shoved Bertoran's body out of the way and hovered around the monitoring console. Melora felt dirtier and more heartsick than ever—there was no joy in her mind, no thoughts of victory. Her world was still endangered, she was estranged from her crew and the man she loved, and she had killed a fellow Elaysian.

A Jeptah's shoulders slumped, and he turned back to her. "Levels have increased. The fractal and darkmatter programs still do not respond. There has been widespread destruction to the healthy crystals."

"All right," she said, "it's time to stop pretending that we know everything. We tried Tangre Bertoran's way, and it failed. If the Starfleet crew will still help us, it's time to try their plan. I will atone the rest of my life for what I have done here, but that's between me and the shade of my father."

The two Jeptah nodded in agreement, although they still looked shocked beyond belief. Melora knew how they felt, because she was numb in her body and sick in her soul. Her mind was fogged by grief over all she had lost, but she knew what had to be done.

"Contact the *Enterprise*," she said. "They have the crystal keys—they are the rightful proxies for the senior engineers. But leave me out of it . . . I've done enough."

The Jeptah didn't argue with that, and even the Frill and the Alpusta moved out of her way as she flew from the monitoring room.

"The worst of the vibrations appear to be over," reported Data as he carefully maneuvered the shuttlecraft between the massive chunks of multicolored crystal littering the sky. They reminded Captain Picard of cross-sections of giant redwood trees he had seen in California, fallen centuries ago. Some of the prisms were broken so cleanly into such perfect cylinders that they looked like pieces of a crystalline space station floating in outer space.

Aboard the shuttlecraft, they hadn't felt the tremor that had shaken Gemworld to it roots, but they could see its effects. If that happened again—whatever it was—there wouldn't be enough left of the planet to worry about.

The captain looked down at Deanna Troi, still cradled in his lap like a sleeping baby. But she wasn't sleeping, she was in a coma, with low levels of brain activity, according to the medical tricorder. Barclay and Nordine hovered nearby like worried nurses, ready to administer another hypo or take her temperature, but they had done all they could to bring Troi back to consciousness.

Picard wanted to turn around and make straight for the ship, but he had promised Deanna that if she suffered another attack, he would take her to the Gendlii. They had been heading toward the Gendlii anyway, which seemed propitious. He almost dreaded Riker contacting them, because then he would have to tell him about Troi's condition. Since the *Enterprise* hadn't contacted them again, he assumed they had their hands full.

"Data," said the captain, "how much farther to the Gendlii?"

"I expected to reach it by now," answered the android. "But we have been delayed by the debris. I also note that thoron radiation is reaching critical levels in some areas. We certainly have less than four days left before life becomes untenable here."

"That reminds me," said Picard with a heavy sigh. "Mr. Data, if all of our efforts fail, you will be the sole survivor on Gemworld. In that case, we would have to assume the rift is still open, and Starfleet can't be of any help."

The android nodded. "In which case, Captain, I will continue to explore likely remedies to the situation. Although," he added, "it will be lonely."

"Your shields won't protect you on the ship?" asked Keefe Nordine.

"No, the thoron radiation will be so pervasive, it will degrade the shields," answered Data.

"It's possible," said Picard, "that we could make a last-ditch effort to leave the planet and escape from the rift. Judging from past experience, we probably wouldn't make it."

"I estimate a less than a one-in-one-thousand chance," suggested Data. "The rift is obviously growing in destructive power."

"Damn," muttered Keefe Nordine. "Will those idiots ever listen to us?"

The captain sighed. "We've tried. Maybe now they will."

"There's the Gendlii!" said Reg Barclay excitedly, pointing out the window.

The shuttlecraft zoomed around a cloud of broken crystal and banked toward the gigantic cluster covered in a shroud of white mottled with black streaks. Somehow the protective covering of fungus had held the cluster intact while many around it had crumbled.

"Should I try to find the attendants?" asked Data.

"No, we know how to communicate with the

Gendlii," said Picard. "The problem is that Counselor Troi can't eat the fungus in her condition."

"I have considered that," answered Data. "Using our hand phasers, we can vaporize a sample of fungus and collect the vapors when they condense into a liquid. In this way, we can administer the fungus in a hypo."

"Make it so," answered Picard, glad to have the quick-thinking android along. He looked down at the unconscious figure in his lap, feeling helpless. "Let's act quickly."

Deanna Troi floated in darkness, uncertain whether she was dead or merely badly damaged. She knew she was in the thrall of a power much greater than herself, and it was holding her in suspension. It could release her, or it could explode her brain cells and leave her a mindless vegetable. Perhaps it would never let go. It might just keep gripping her mind like a baby with a shiny new plaything.

At least it was no longer angry, and her fear subsided in varying degrees the more she floated without change in this dark netherworld. When the entity felt anger, it lashed out in every direction it had probed with its long tentacles, and her mind was one of those directions. The threat was over—it had been dealt with—and she was just one of the casualties. The window to the other world stayed open, letting the dark shine through.

Now that she recognized the entity, would it recognize her? The communication with the Lipuls had started in one direction only—theirs—but she had eventually succeeded in forcing them to answer her questions. She hadn't asked her questions in so many words—it was more of a desire in her heart that they had read. The same openness which had attracted the Lipuls and the thing from the rift now had to serve as her voice. She couldn't speak, but she could *dream*. With all her being, she could desire to understand.

Despite the limbo in which she floated, Deanna tried to calm herself and recall her life. It was a life spent trying to help and understand others, and she had often fought through personal problems and conflicting emotions to do her job. If she had to die now, it would be with great sorrow but a clear conscience. *This is the way I am!* Deanna wanted to shout. *I hold no malice toward you.*

A shiny bit of light intruded on her vision, like a flash of lightning outside the window of a dark room. She gasped as her body was lifted up and flung into a swirling whirlpool of flashing light.

Her body was released in the void to drift . . . she knew she had traveled a great distance . . . and at the same time no distance at all. She was in another place, different from any plane of existence she had ever known, yet it was a place she had been before. *When?* She wracked her brain, and knew that she had been here in a dream. She had traveled here with the Lipuls.

It was the other dimension, where there was such a multitude of life. The Lipuls had known that coming here was dangerous and selfish—an invasion—but it was such a short trip, they could not resist going back again and again. They discovered a way to sample DNA from creatures in the other dimension, memorize the sequences, and duplicate those creatures in laboratories. They were able to pick and choose from among the multitude of life in the other place, selecting those species that could best survive the changing conditions on Gemworld.

They were no longer lonely, but they had stolen something of great value—life. And they had awakened a force of great power and potential. It learned from them, though they never wanted to teach it. Once they realized what they were creating, the Lipuls backed off. They sent their dreamships far and wide, but they never crossed the dimensions again. Still, it was too late; the thing they had awakened had learned all it needed to know. And it had bided its time, for time meant even less to the entity than it did to the Lipuls.

Deanna knew all of this in an instant, yet her mind kept filling with questions. The nature of evil it did not understand. . . . It only understood what it had observed and learned from the observation. Deanna knew that the Lipuls had been poor teachers, setting an example that would come back to haunt them a hundredfold.

As her mind filled with all the grievances and quandaries of an ageless intelligence, Deanna felt her own mind slipping away. She had no way to close the floodgate any more than they could close the rift. It just kept pouring into her consciousness, like the darkmatter flooding Gemworld. Once again, she could see the black pool opening beneath her feet, drawing her in . . . overwhelming her with fear and futility.

I can't take any more! she screamed in her mind, slamming her fist against the swirling wall of darkness. The pain jolted her—it was *real!* Her hand burned, and the blood seemed to boil from her fingertips.

But the pain subsided, and she felt herself slipping

again into the utter bleakness of the alien intelligence. Deanna tried to embrace the pain to hold onto her sanity, but her mind was no match for the all-consuming entity. It was going to swallow her whole.

"You are not alone," said a sudden voice. "Remember all you have to live for. I know the singularity that has entered your mind. I will call it 'Father.' It does not want *you;* you are only the messenger. Father must leave, because it doesn't belong here—and you don't belong here. Even if it destroys its children, we forgive it. Father doesn't need you, but Will, Lwaxana, Jean-Luc, Reg, Beverly, and so many others *do* need you."

Their images filled her mind—her friends, family, shipmates. Encouraged by the soothing voice, she began to put the fear out of her mind, and the swirling whirlpool beneath her feet began to contract like a planet fading into the distance. As she clung with joy to the images of her life, the darkness evaporated like a mist.

"Smelling salts," said a voice. "Quickly."

Pungent aromas stabbed her senses, making her recoil and sneeze. With a feeling that a mask was lifting from her face, Deanna peeled her eyes open. She blinked, trying to focus on the happy faces staring at her. At first she thought they were the same friendly faces from her dream, but their laughing voices told her that they were more real than that.

"Welcome back!" crowed Reg Barclay.

"Yes, indeed, welcome back," said Captain Picard with a relieved smile.

"You had us sweating, Counselor," said Keefe Nordine with a wink.

The floating sensation was also real, and she looked around to find herself surrounded by a massive fungus, which coated everything like a blanket of fresh snow. She could see a spot of blood on the fungus, and another place where a chunk had been broken off. A few meters away floated their battered but beautiful shuttlecraft.

Weakly, she squeezed Captain Picard's hand. "Thank you . . . for bringing me back here."

"I always keep a promise if I can," answered the captain. "Thank Data, he was the one who figured out how to allow you to communicate with the Gendlii."

"Thank you, Data," she said, looking for the android. She finally spotted him floating halfway between the fungus and the shuttlecraft. The android's head was cocked quizzically, and he seemed to be listening to a distant noise only he could hear.

"This area is not secure," declared the android. Extending his arm, he reached for a rung on the shuttlecraft and pulled himself into the open hatch. He immediately fell to work on the shuttle's controls.

A moment later, Deanna heard a buzzing sound that she had heard before, and she twisted around and reached for the captain's arm. "Sir, they're coming! They're—"

"They're here!" cried Reg Barclay as a horde of Frills swarmed over the lip of the Gendlii, their wings buzzing and their jaws snapping. From below them, an army of chittering Alpusta came bouncing up the side of the fungus-covered prism. Within seconds, they were surrounded by hundreds of nonhumanoid creatures, who filled the sky and crowded toward them ominously.

Data appeared in the hatchway, holding a phaser rifle. He looked expectantly at the captain, but Picard waved his hands in the face of overwhelming numbers.

"Put down the weapon," said Picard grimly. "We'll surrender."

Reluctantly, Data put down the phaser rifle, and a phalanx of Alpusta moved steadily toward them.

Chapter Fourteen

WITH A GIGANTIC FUNGUS at his back and nowhere to run, Reg Barclay stared at the Frills and Alpusta massing in the sky. The Frills appeared agitated, curling back and forth in the sky with powerful thrusts of their delicate wings, while the Alpusta bounced on their webs, looking for places to roost in the soft fungus.

Reg was floating helplessly, too far from the shuttlecraft to duck inside. Although Captain Picard had offered to surrender to this overwhelming force, it wasn't clear they would accept. After the terrifying tremblor that had just shaken Gemworld, these particular inhabitants looked angrier than ever. All Reg wished was that he could see Melora again before he died.

"Yerjakzik!" shouted Keefe Nordine behind him. "Old friend, it's good to see you!"

A venerable silver-backed Frill broke from the teeming horde and cruised toward the outsiders. Reg tried not to duck in fear, but the sinewy predator had to be three meters in length if it was a centimeter. It stopped in front of them and reared back like a cobra, then it fluttered its wings in an eerie approximation of a voice.

"We have sought you far and wide," declared the Frill. "The crisis grows worse, and our brothers are at a loss. Our brother the Alpusta is ready to recognize the chosen proxy of the Elaysians."

Reg didn't realize the Frill was talking about *him*, until one of the spidery Alpusta bobbed forward on its long retractable web. That was when he saw the dark blue shard hanging on a strand of web from its spiny body.

"Get it, Reg!" said Nordine, pushing him forward.

With a brave smile plastered to his face, Barclay approached the fearsome beast. After all they had been through, he still half-expected this gesture to be a trick. However, the great Alpusta folded its spindly legs and seemed to bow. This allowed Reg to remove the crystal from its headless torso. The strand of old webbing felt like a slimy rubber band in his hand, nevertheless he put it reverently around his neck, adding to his collection.

The engineer felt as if he had to say something to end the impromptu ceremony, so he declared loudly, "I will use this precious key to save Gemworld!"

That seemed to meet with approval, because the Frills turned tail and began to disperse, and the Alpusta shrank away from him, descending rapidly on their long webs. Reg remained perfectly still while the skies in front of the Gendlii emptied of these hundreds of remarkable life-forms. As suddenly as they had appeared, they were gone.

Reg finally let out a pent-up breath and looked at the captain, who was regarding him with similar respect. "Well done, Mr. Barclay. I don't know if it will help us, but now we have all six crystals. I'd better try to contact the *Enterprise* again."

He tapped his combadge. "Picard to *Enterprise*."

"Riker here," answered a familiar voice. "Is everything all right?"

"Yes, Number One, everything is all right, considering."

"Sorry it's taken so long to get back to you," said the first officer, "but we've been negotiating with the Jeptah."

"Good," said the captain with relief. "You finally got through to them."

"Believe it or not, they contacted *us*," answered Riker. "It's taken a while to sort through their demands, but I think we're finally ready to try our original plan— to shut down the shell and power the forcefields from here."

"What about Tangre Bertoran's opposition?"

"He doesn't seem to be in the picture anymore," answered Riker. "I guess they had enough of him after that stupid attempt to blast the rift with phasers."

The captain frowned. "I suppose we ought to be glad it didn't turn out worse than it did. But you'll have to proceed with caution, Number One."

"Don't worry about that, sir. We made some demands, too. They have to return the phaser bank they stole, and we're sending over La Forge to make sure they don't hijack the ship when they put us under their forcefields. So we're right back where we started, minus Tangre Bertoran. Believe me, we're dealing with a lot of sadder-but-wiser Jeptah."

"We've been successful, too. We have the last of the six crystals and we'll be heading back as soon as we can. But it will still be eight to ten hours before we reach you."

"No problem, sir," anwered Riker. "We'll try to be all set up by the time you get here. By the way, there's no word from Melora Pazlar, and the Jeptah refuse to discuss her. We're going to make it one of our conditions that we find out her whereabouts before we proceed."

"Good idea. Picard out." Carefully the captain pushed off from the fungus and drifted toward the shuttlecraft. "Mr. Data, prepare to get under way."

"Yes, sir," answered the android as he returned to the pilot seat and began working the controls.

"Thank goodness," muttered Reg. He felt a hand touch his arm, and he turned to see Deanna Troi, smiling at him.

"You look good in jewelry," she said, pointing to the collection of crystal shards floating from his neck. "It's time to give you one more." Gingerly she took the Lipuls' clear crystal from her neck and draped it around his crowded neck.

"But they chose *you*," protested Reg.

"And I choose you," she answered. "I'm going to withdraw from giving further aid to Gemworld. It's been too hard on me—I need to check into sickbay for a nice long rest."

"Don't we all," said Reg with a sigh. Then his expression grew worried. "What do you think happened to Melora?"

"I don't know," admitted Troi. "It sounds like *somebody* talked some sense into the Jeptah—maybe it was she."

Reg nodded solemnly, taking some solace from that remark. Wherever Melora was, he knew she was speaking her mind and trying to help her people, but he was still in despair over her absence. Without her he felt abandoned and alone, despite the presence of his shipmates.

"All aboard!" shouted Captain Picard from the open hatch. He tossed a rope toward the aged fungus, and Barclay, Troi, and Keefe Nordine caught hold and pulled themselves up to the waiting shuttlecraft.

Although Barclay had dozed off on the cramped shuttlecraft, as Data piloted them back to the *Enterprise,* he still felt drained when he stepped off the craft. There were two welcoming parties waiting for them in the main shuttlebay: a med team from sickbay to take charge of Deanna Troi and Keefe Nordine, and an engineering team led by Geordi La Forge.

After all they had been through together, Reg hated to be separated from Troi, but he could see that the counselor was still weak and distracted from her ordeal. Nordine was cheerful, giving them all handshakes and words of encouragement as they wheeled him away. Captain Picard once again thanked the young civilian, promising to help him any way he could.

"Just save this weird planet," muttered Nordine. "I want to come back here sometime—for a *short* visit!"

"We'll do our best," answered Picard. The captain turned to La Forge. "What's our status?"

"Our main power grid is patched into their transfer conduits," answered La Forge, "and we're operating at acceptable levels under their forcefield. The Jeptah have been amazingly cooperative—*this* time around. All we need to do is plug in your six crystals and shut down the shell. All darkmatter collection, all fractal generation, everything but the forcefields should stop. When we restart a few seconds later, the programming should be back at default levels. We've gone over everything; it should work, but I wouldn't mind if Data were on the bridge to oversee the power transfer."

The android nodded in agreement. "With your permission, Captain."

"Go ahead, Data."

The android strode briskly toward the exit, and the rest of them fell into line behind the captain. Reg sidled up to La Forge and cleared his throat. "Um, excuse me, sir, did you hear anything about Lieutenant Pazlar?"

Geordi winced painfully. "Uh, yeah, Reg, we did. I'm afraid it's not good news. Captain, you should hear this, too."

Picard stopped and looked expectantly at the chief engineer, while Reg twisted his hands nervously.

"The Jeptah weren't going to tell us anything," began La Forge, "but we made them talk. Apparently, they brought Lieutenant Pazlar back to the shell, and she was present when they shot our phasers at the rift. I don't know exactly what happened, but they said that she attacked Tangre Bertoran . . . and killed him."

Barclay gasped and put his hand to his mouth. *"Killed* him?"

"She's got a temper, Reg," said Geordi softly. "I can't say that we're mourning the loss of Tangre Bertoran very much, but the Jeptah are. I believe they've already taken his body to the Blood Prism . . . to give him to the Frills."

"W-Where is Melora?" demanded Barclay.

"Nobody knows. They don't know." La Forge sighed and shook his head. "I gather that this killing is a very serious matter, and she'll probably go back to her enclave, where they'll decide her fate. I'm sorry, Reg."

Barclay's lower lip quivered, and his innards felt as if they were turning into black marrow, like the inside of a rotting crystal. His legs were already wobbly from all the time spent in low gravity, and now they began to buckle. But before Reg could stumble he felt a strong hand on his shoulder, holding him up.

He turned to see Captain Picard, looking sympathetic but determined. "Buck up, Mr. Barclay. Remember that Lieutenant Pazlar *chose* to get involved, and to involve all of us. If we falter now, we fail her most of all. Let's put our personal feelings aside and finish the job she started."

"Yes, sir," answered Barclay, forcing his slumped shoulders to attention. "I have to go to security and get the real shards."

"These aren't the real ones?" asked La Forge, looking at the sparkling collection hanging from Reg's neck like giant teeth in a primitive necklace.

"Some of them are," answered Reg, separating out the clear one, the dark blue, and the amber shard wrapped in ribbons. "The ones we got on our latest trip—these, from the Lipuls, Alpusta, and Yilterns—are real. But the other three are replicas. I hope the originals are still in storage. I put them in a security vault."

"If they had forcefields protecting them," said La Forge, "they're probably okay."

"That's our next stop," said Picard. "By the way, Mr. La Forge, good job on recapturing the ship. I heard that was mostly your staff."

"Right place at the right time," said La Forge with a smile. "I keep telling people the engine room is the safest place to work, but they never listen. Do they, Reg?"

"Hmmm? Oh, yes, sir," muttered Barclay absently, having only been half-listening.

"You'll see her again," said La Forge with false cheer. "Nobody on Gemworld is going to refuse you anything—aren't you the king of the proxies?"

"I guess so," answered Reg, managing a smile, but he didn't feel like the king of anything.

Reg stayed mostly in a fog of worry as he accompanied the captain, La Forge, and two other engineers to the security stronghold on deck 10. This was part bunker, part office, like a police station in the middle of a city, and manned by strong-jawed security types. The brig was located here, as well as vaults of various sizes for stowing materials that were deemed sensitive or valuable. The crewmembers didn't use these facilities much, trusting the security of their quarters, but visiting dignitaries and passengers couldn't resist the sense of added security.

The captain himself retrieved the three original shards entrusted by the inhabitants of Gemworld to Barclay. There was the violet one from the Elaysians, bequeathed by Zuka Juno before his murder; the Gendlii's emerald-green gem, which Tangre Bertoran had considered his own; and the blood-red crystal from the Frills.

Reg handed over the replicas, which they entrusted back to the vault, and Captain Picard took command of all six crystal keys. Although he should have felt relieved at handing over these priceless relics, Reg felt somewhat diminished. First he had lost Melora, and now he was losing the crystals—everything special that had happened to him was slipping away.

He dutifully followed Captain Picard, La Forge, and the others to the transporter room, and he hardly felt any apprehension when they beamed over to the shell. After everything he had been through, what was having his molecules scrambled for a few seconds? His heart was already scrambled beyond repair.

They were met in a broad circular corridor by a solemn cadre of yellow-garbed Elaysians, with one well-behaved Alpusta lurking in the rear. Reg was beginning to realize that the Alpusta had rampaged rather severely through the *Enterprise,* and that they were now seeking forgiveness in their own way.

"I am Hako Fezdan," said a thin, humorless Elaysian. He pointed to his Alpusta colleague. "If need be, we have technicians who can check the connections outside the shell, but all of our instruments indicate that everything is in readiness."

"Let's hope so," said Picard impatiently. "Readings

we took from the shuttlecraft show that thoron radiation is increasing all over Gemworld. We need to get this done."

The Jeptah bowed. "We are in complete agreement with you, Captain Picard. May I express our profound regret over the incident precipitated by our late leader, Tangre Bertoran."

"Acknowledged," answered Picard brusquely, sounding as if he wasn't entirely ready to forgive them yet. "Where is the Termination Link?"

"This way, Captain. Please hold hands."

Once again, the outsiders linked hands like schoolchildren and were pulled along, gliding weightlessly through the silent corridors. Reg wondered where everybody had gone, and he decided that most of them had returned to their enclaves for the end, whatever it turned out to be. They finally reached the vaulted door of the programming room where the Lipul had viciously murdered Zuka Juno, but they didn't enter that hallowed chamber. Instead Hako Fezdan reached under the door and slid open a small secret panel that had been disguised to look like a latch hook.

At once, a larger secret panel slid open above their heads, revealing a dark and musty-smelling chamber. In fact, the dust of millennia spewed out, causing Reg to sneeze violently. The Alpusta recoiled from his unexpected outburst, its legs clattering against the back wall.

"Sorry," said Reg, rubbing his nose.

The Elaysian bowed apologetically. "As you can see, the Termination Link has never been used, and was never *expected* to be used. I believe only four of us will fit. That will be you, Captain, the proxy, myself, and Commander La Forge."

"Fine," said the captain curtly.

Reg wanted to excuse himself, not liking such dark, tight, dusty places, but he was the proxy. It was his duty to see this thing through to the end. One more sacrifice he would make for Gemworld.

Hako Fezdan pushed off the floor and drifted upward into the dark chamber. He extended a hand down and pulled the captain, La Forge, and Barclay after him.

To Reg's surprise, though the interior of the hidden chamber was cramped it was also spectacular. The walls were made entirely of yellow crystal the color of the sun. Fine strands of wires and miniature circuits were embedded inside the transparent material, and all the wires led to six hexagonal openings, marked not by colors but by shapes denoting the six sentient species of Gemworld.

Below them, in the corridor, one of the Elaysians was weeping openly, and even Hako Fezdan looked ashen as he considered the gravity of what they were about to do. His voice wavered as he spoke: "There is a ceremony that accompanies this procedure. . . ."

"Does it make any difference as to the effectiveness?" asked Picard.

"No," admitted the Jeptah. "But the Holy Shards must be inserted in order from left to right. Upon the insertion of the last one, the shard of the Lipuls, the Termination Link will be complete, and the shell will cease. When the shards are removed, the shell will resume operation."

"Let's do it," said La Forge. "I'll alert Data." He tapped him combadge. "La Forge to Data."

"Data here," came the efficient reply.

"We're ready. How about you?"

"Your preparations appear to be thorough as usual," answered the android. "We are ready to transfer power to the shell's forcefields."

"Okay," said La Forge, "I'll give you a countdown of five." He pointed to Picard, who lifted the first shard and inserted it into the leftmost receptacle. Dull circuits embedded inside the yellow crystal suddenly glowed brightly.

"Five," intoned La Forge.

Picard inserted another shard, and La Forge said, "Four."

The violet crystal which Reg had worn for so many days was inserted next, and La Forge counted, "Three."

When the next crystal was inserted, he said, "Two."

With difficulty, Picard plugged in the amber crystal wrapped in ribbons, and La Forge intoned, "One." Only one slot now remained empty.

"Transferring power," reported Data. "Transfer complete—forcefields operating as normal."

The Elaysian stared down the hatch at his compatriots, and one of them happily confirmed, "Forcefields are on."

With a firm push, Captain Picard inserted the last crystal shard in the Termination Link, and everyone held his breath.

Nothing happened. At least, nothing in the shell changed in their immediate vicinity. The humans looked quizzically at the Elaysian, who could only shake his head in amazement.

"It . . . it should be off!" he insisted.

"Data," said La Forge, "do you register any change in the shell?"

"No," answered the android, "although the shell is attempting to compensate for the added power influx. Please advise."

Angrily, Picard pulled all the shards out and firmly reinserted them . . . with absolutely no effect.

"Oh, no," muttered Barclay, feeling a worse churning in his stomach than ever before. "I think I know what happened."

"What?" demanded the captain.

Reg gulped. "When I replicated the first three shards, I noticed that the one Tangre Bertoran gave me had a slightly different composition from the others. I didn't think anything about it at the time, because I didn't know much about them. But what if he gave me a fake?"

"That idiot!" muttered La Forge, slapping his fist into his palm. "Even dead he screws us up."

Picard turned angrily to Hako Fezdan. "Is that possible? Do you know anything about this?"

The Elaysian recoiled from the captain's wrath. "He didn't always take us into his confidence. But—yes—it is possible . . . he was vehemently opposed to shutting down the shell."

"*Enterprise* to away team," came Riker's insistent voice. "We don't read any change in the shell, and we're almost on overload. What's going on?"

"We couldn't shut it down," grumbled the captain. "Cease the power transfer."

"Yes, sir."

Captain Picard grabbed the Elaysian by his robe and shook him. "I want you to go to Bertoran's quarters, his office, any place he might have hidden that shard—and *find it!*"

"Y-Yes, sir!" whispered the Elaysian. He flew from the chamber, leaving Picard, La Forge, and Barclay alone . . . and helpless to prevent a colossal catastrophe.

Below them, the Elaysian continued to weep. Reg would have joined him, except he was too numb and shocked to cry.

Chapter Fifteen

DEANNA TROI FELT THEIR PRESENCE before she heard their voices. Actually it was Beverly Crusher's angry voice she heard first, defending the sanctity of her sickbay.

"I won't allow it!" insisted Beverly. "She's exhausted, she's suffering from amnesia, shock, and trauma. She needs bed rest for at least forty-eight hours. Those are my orders."

"We haven't got forty-eight hours," said Captain Picard with an uncharacteristic lack of patience. "Please, Beverly, let us see her."

Deanna sat up in her bed and didn't feel too bad, only tired. Grabbing a robe and wrapping it around her shivering body, she crawled out of bed and walked to the door of her private room. Through the window, she could see the captain and Reg Barclay confronting the angry doctor.

"Jean-Luc, don't make me call security and have you thrown out of here," warned Crusher. "You leave my patient alone."

Deanna pressed a panel and opened the door. "It's all right, Beverly. I can see them."

Now Crusher turned on her. "Excuse me, but in sickbay I don't take orders from captains *or* patients. Now you get back into that bed."

"We're all going to die, aren't we?" asked Troi, reading the deep creases on the captain's face.

"Yes, there's a very good chance we're all going to die," admitted Picard, stepping toward her. "At the very least, everyone on Gemworld is going to die. We'll probably try to make a break for it in the *Enterprise,* but Data gives us a one-in-a-thousand chance of escaping from the rift."

Crusher heaved her shoulders and shook her head. "And you think this one sick woman is going to save everybody?"

"She's our only chance," answered Picard.

With that grim assessment, Beverly ushered the visitors into Deanna's room and shut the door behind them. The doctor stood with her arms crossed as Deanna climbed back into her bed. Picard and Barclay waited patiently, although Reg was wringing his hands.

"You weren't able to shut down the shell?" asked Troi.

"No," answered the captain. "One of the shards was fake. Without it we can't shut down the shell, unless we blow it up with our weapons. That would kill the inhabitants as surely as the rift."

Deanna pulled the covers up around her chin. "You want me to contact the entity . . . and ask it to withdraw."

"I object," said Crusher. "She's not up to that. It's extremely dangerous."

"Then you can watch your sickbay fill up with cases of thoron radiation poisoning," replied Picard. "Believe me, I wish we had an alternative—but we don't."

"Beverly, you can keep me under watch," said Deanna with a brave smile. "I'd like to try it. So far, the entity has only come after me—it'll be surprised when I go after *it*."

The doctor raised her hands in resignation. "All right, we'll put the monitors on you." She stepped behind the bed and turned on the array of electronic graphs and charts, which beeped and blinked ominously.

Crusher turned and looked at the two visitors. "Are you going to stand there and stare at her while she does this?"

"No," answered Picard. "Good luck, Counselor." The captain started for the door, but Barclay hesitated for a moment.

"You've always told me there is good in all of us," said Reg, "even when we're doing bad things. I know that was true in *my* case, when I was doing that stuff on the holodeck. Try to find the good that's out there."

"I will," promised Troi. "I heard about Melora—I'm sorry."

Reg lifted his chin bravely. "We'll see her again . . . soon."

"We'll try." Troi kept up a brave smile, too, until Picard and Barclay were gone. Then the enormity of her task hit her, and she shrank into her bedcovers.

Beverly shook her head forlornly. "I'll be monitoring you from sickbay." She looked as if she wanted to say more, but what was there to say? The doctor turned on her heel and marched out, leaving Deanna alone.

The Betazoid settled back in her bed and tried to clear her mind. She knew what the rift looked like, because she had seen it. Lying in bed, this time in control, she looked at the ceiling and tried to imagine that awful black gash appearing from nowhere. For the first time, she *willed* it to come, the jagged chasm of darkness.

She stared so long at the blank ceiling that gradually a tear began to form. As she stared in fascination, the black rip in the ceiling grew larger and oddly three-dimensional, as if something were punching its way through the hull. This time, Deanna didn't flinch or scream; she lifted her arms to welcome the apparition. Slowly it turned into a swirling pool of ink that drew her in, pulling her mind into its dark, impenetrable depths.

Without fear, she opened her mind and floated into the entity's black realm. It was hard to say what dimension this was, as the entity spanned both; maybe it spanned a *hundred* dimensions, she thought suddenly. Deanna imagined it was a kind of gatekeeper that tried to guard the precious life on the other side. That's why it was so angry at the Lipuls and their selfish thievery.

With a start, she realized that the gatekeeper was

seeking forgiveness for its failure to protect the lives entrusted to it. Its destructive attack on Gemworld had been purely defensive in nature, even though the wrongs had occurred billions of years ago. It had taken the entity a long time to perfect the sort of astral travel the Lipuls performed so effortlessly. Only then had the gatekeeper seen the full extent of the Lipuls' thievery and the true purpose behind their repeated visits.

Are any of the other species native to Gemworld? she asked in her mind.

Only the Frills.

With that brief answer, Troi realized that she had made contact. There was no reason not to speak her mind, because there would not be another chance.

"Gatekeeper," she began, "you have performed your job valiantly. You are to be commended. The beings which the Lipuls have transplanted to Gemworld are happy and content and do not know that they come from your realm. If they know, it does not matter, because they are like you, able to prosper anywhere. They are the greatest of your children, for they shine their light in two worlds. You need not suffer guilt—you have done all you can to protect the life entrusted to you."

Thieves! came the vehement answer. *They must be punished.*

"They have been punished," insisted Troi. "Their realm is in ruins, and you have invaded their most precious place, their dreams. But now if you stay in this realm, if you keep the rift open, you will kill all of your children. The guilty Lipuls will survive in their prisms, but the innocent—the Elaysians, Alpusta, Gendlii, and Yilterns—will die."

They must not invade.

She went on, "You don't realize how long ago the Lipuls came, because time means so little to you. The Lipuls have not journeyed to your dimension for ages beyond measure, longer than my species has been alive. They are afraid of you, now more so than ever. If you withdraw now, you will be the victor. Generations on this side will praise not just your majesty but your compassion. You will be forgiven the destruction, which was not your fault.

"Please," she begged, "it is time for you to go. Close the rift, and they will never invade again. If you go now, all will be forgiven, and your children will live."

Deanna closed her eyes, wondering if she would lose her life—or only her sanity. Right now she felt as if she could come out of this floating trance, but not if the gatekeeper retaliated. She strained to hear an answer, but all she felt was a single urge:

Sleep.

When Deanna Troi finally woke up, she felt so groggy that for a moment she thought she was floating near the Gendlii. In fact, she saw the same familiar face the Gendlii had shown to her, and he said the same thing:

"Imzadi." Will Riker gave her a beaming smile that was filled with love.

She reached up and touched his clean-shaven cheek, which didn't feel like a giant fungus. "Imzadi," she breathed.

He took her hand and kissed it, and the warmth of

his lips told her this wasn't a dream. With a start, she opened her eyes wide and saw the face of her beloved.

"I'm awake," she said with surprise. "How long have I been asleep?"

Riker turned to look at Beverly Crusher, who stood in the doorway, smiling. "Almost twenty hours."

"Twenty hours?" asked Troi in shock. "But the thoron radiation . . . the rift!"

"The rift is gone," replied Will. "It closed up nineteen hours ago. I don't think that was a coincidence, do you?"

A slight figure hobbled past the door and stuck his head in. It was Keefe Nordine. "Ah, Counselor, welcome back to the land of the living! Is it true that all you did was ask the rift to close up and go away?"

With a satisfied sigh, Deanna sank back in her bed. "Yes. But I had to forgive it first."

"Forgive it?" asked Will.

Deanna squeezed his hand. "As a friend once told me, that's all any of us are looking for—forgiveness."

Reg Barclay was nervous as he and Captain Picard materialized near an Elaysian enclave at the crux of a giant blue cluster, and it wasn't because of his usual fear of transporting. He was nervous because he was finally going to see Melora again, or so he hoped. Reports had come in from a reconnaissance team that she had been sighted in her home enclave. Reg was relieved to see that the destruction here wasn't too bad, and the nets and ropes still maintained a semblance of the housing he had seen on their earlier visit. That had been only a few days ago, but it seemed like a lifetime.

On that earlier trip Melora had been treated like a returning hero, and now it was their turn, as happy Elaysians gathered around them. Reg and the captain had spent the last ten hours returning the Holy Shards to their rightful owners, saying good-bye to the unique species of Gemworld. They had even retrieved their shuttlecraft from the grateful Yilterns, plus other small gifts.

Now they had one last shard to return, the violet one given him by Zuka Juno. They could have given it to the Jeptah on the shell, but somehow it seemed better to give it to the common people, the ones who would have to choose a new senior engineer.

Reg scanned the crowd of clamoring well-wishers, looking in vain for Melora. He was glad that the captain was so adept at diplomatic chores, because the captain could deal with the press of people and their questions. The *Enterprise* had to leave, Picard explained patiently for the sixth time, but a fleet of relief ships was on its way to help them rebuild their planet and remove the mutant crystal. Already the thoron radiation had diminished greatly.

Finally Barclay saw someone in the crowd he recognized, the woman named Dupanza, whom Melora had considered her favorite parent among the hundreds who had raised her in the communal setting. He grabbed the captain's arm and pointed Dupanza out to him. When the older woman tried to escape into the layers of netting, Reg put his celebrity status to good use.

"Dupanza!" he yelled. "I must speak with her! Please, bring her to me."

None could refuse the hero and super-proxy of Gemworld, and Dupanza was soon ushered into their presence. Reg could tell from her lowered eyes that she knew where Melora was. He didn't pry for answers right away; instead he took the violet shard from his neck and presented it to her.

"Here, please keep this for your people until they can choose a new senior engineer," he said, to cheers from the crowd.

Despite her reticence, Dupanza was forced to be gracious and take the crystal, to more cheers. When he got a chance, he whispered into her ear, "Please take us to Melora. I have to see her, and the captain has to know her plans."

"She's in seclusion," answered Dupanza.

"We could do a scan for her and transport her to the ship," said Captain Picard. "She's still under my command."

"Oh, very well," said Dupanza with resignation. "Link up and follow me."

Dupanza conducted the two visitors deep into the nets that made up the storerooms and living quarters of the enclave. The other Elaysians seemed to realize that this was a private matter, and they drifted off to their chores.

They found Melora at the deepest crux of the crystal, curled in a dark crevice. When she saw them, she uncurled from her hiding place and flew reluctantly out to meet them. Although Reg still considered her to be beautiful, she looked wan and tired. The fiery spirit he had grown to love was gone, replaced by an air of penitence and grief.

He held out his hands to her. "Melora! We were successful, thanks to you and Commander Troi!"

"Thanks to Commander Troi perhaps," she admitted

gloomily. She didn't take his hands, and he was forced to let them hang limply at his sides.

Captain Picard spoke bluntly, "Lieutenant Pazlar, you are still under my command. Can you explain why you haven't reported for duty?"

"I can't go back," she answered. "You must know by now that I killed Tangre Bertoran."

"I'm sure it was an accident," declared Reg.

"It was no accident—it was my anger, which I've never learned to control." She met the captain's gaze with her crystal-blue eyes. "Captain, I must atone for what I've done, and that means solitude and reflection for many shadow marks. My family and the Exalted Ones will then meet to discuss my fate. I know this is a time of great rejoicing all over Gemworld, but I can't take part in that. And I can't simply return to my duties as if nothing has happened."

Melora squared her shoulders, looking momentarily like the Starfleet officer she had been for ten years. "Captain, I respectfully request a leave of absence for an unlimited period of time."

Picard scowled. "I hate to lose a good officer, and you *are* a good officer, but I won't force you to return. On my official report, I'll say that you're staying here to help rebuild your world. I hope at some point in the future you'll realize that you have a family other than this one, and that we need you too."

He held out his hand. "Good-bye, Lieutenant Pazlar. The door is always open for you in Starfleet."

She smiled slightly as she took his hand. "Thank you, sir. It was a pleasure serving on the finest ship in the fleet."

"Lieutenant Barclay," said the captain, "I'm going to give you a few minutes alone—but don't take too long."

"Yes, sir," answered Reg gloomily.

Using the nets to pull himself along, the captain exited from the shadowy crevice at the rear of the enclave. Reg could contain himself no longer, and he reached out and grabbed Melora, pulling her slim body to his chest. At first she resisted, but then she gripped him in quiet desperation. For several seconds, they clung to each other like two drowning people with one life vest between them.

"I can't live without you," pleaded Barclay. "You've got to come back."

"Oh, Reg, don't make it worse," she said tearfully, not looking into his eyes. "How would we live? *Where* would we live? Even if I hadn't killed him, I don't know if I could leave Gemworld now. Look how much work there is to do."

"Then I'll get a leave of absence, too," he declared. "I'll stay here with you, and we'll—"

She touched his lips tenderly to stop his flood of words. "And you'll let your legs atrophy, as well as your mind? No, Reg, you're a ship's engineer; you need a ship. Let me do my atonement, which I have to do alone. One of the things I have to figure out is what to do with the rest of my life. I know I'll miss *you,* and I'm curious to see if I'll miss Starfleet, too."

She managed a brave smile through her misty tears. "If we're meant to be, Reg, this won't end it. A part of me will always be with you."

"A part of me will be dead without you," muttered Reg.

She gently pushed him away. "When you get back to the ship, go into my quarters and get my cane. I want you to keep it for me. Then you will have part of me with you."

"I'll be back for the rest of you," vowed Reg, sniffing back his tears.

"I'm counting on it." She kissed him gently on the mouth, then pulled away from him before he could embrace her again. With a push off the crystal wall, Melora flew away into the shadows and was gone.

Reg had composed himself by the time he joined Captain Picard outside, but he was still dazed. He looked around at the lofty prisms reaching for the sky, and he marveled that he was floating in midair.

"Is any of this real?" he asked. "It seems so much like a dream."

"Dreams are real while they last," answered Captain Picard with a sympathetic smile. He tapped his combadge. "Two to beam up."

Then they disappeared in two sparkling columns of light, and their dancing molecules seemed to blend into the flecks of light refracted through the towering crystals of Gemworld.

OUR FIRST SERIAL NOVEL!

Presenting, one chapter per month . . .

**The very beginning of the Starfleet
Adventure . . .**

**STAR TREK®
STARFLEET: YEAR ONE**

A Novel in Twelve Parts

**by
Michael Jan Friedman**

Chapter Seven

Chapter Seven

Weapons Officer Morgan Kelly took a deep breath and considered herself in the full-length mirror.

Like everyone else on the Christopher-class vessel *Peregrine,* she wore an open-collared blue uniform with a black mock-turtle pullover underneath it. A gold Starfleet chevron graced the uniform's left breast, and Kelly's rank of lieutenant was denoted by two gold bands encircling her right sleeve.

She tilted her red-haired head to one side and frowned. She had worn the gold and black of Earth Command for so long she had come to think of it as part of her natural coloring. A blue uniform looked as inappropriate as a hot-pink atomic missile.

But there it was, Kelly mused, her frown deepening. And she would get used to it. She would *have* to.

The sound of chimes brought her out of her reverie. Kelly turned to the double set of sliding doors that separated her quarters from the corridor beyond and wondered who might be calling on her.

Maybe it was the engineer she had met earlier, who had gotten lost looking for the mess hall. Or yet another lieutenant j.g., wondering if she had received her full complement of toiletries. . . .

It couldn't be a friend. After all, the lieutenant only had one of those on the ship . . . and he was waiting for her on the bridge.

"I'm coming," she sighed.

Crossing the room, Kelly pressed the padd in the bulkhead beside the sliding doors and watched them hiss open. They revealed a silver-skinned, ruby-eyed figure in a uniform as blue as her own.

"Captain Cobaryn—?" she said, unable to conceal her surprise.

He inclined his head slightly. "May I come in?"

Kelly hesitated for a moment. Then she realized she really had no choice in the matter. "Of course. But I should tell you, I'm—"

"Due on the bridge in ten minutes," the Rigelian said, finishing her declaration for her. He fashioned a smile, stretching the series of ridges that ran from his temple to his jaw. "I know. I spoke with Captain Shumar before I transported over."

"Did you?" the lieutenant responded, getting the feeling that she had been the victim of some kind of conspiracy. *I'll be the first officer in Starfleet to kill my captain,* she told herself.

"Yes," Cobaryn rejoined. "I wish to speak with you."

Of course you do, she replied inwardly.

After all, Cobaryn had taken every opportunity to speak with her back on Earth Base 14 in the aftermath of the Romulan assault. It hardly came as a shock that he wanted to speak with her *now.*

And he had gone to some pretty great lengths to do so. All six of the fleet's Christophers were supposed to leave Earth orbit in less than an hour, and the Rigelian had a command of his own to attend to. There might even be a regulation prohibiting a captain from leaving his vessel at such a momentous juncture.

If there was, Cobaryn seemed unaware of it ... or else, for the sake of his infatuation with Kelly, he had decided to ignore it.

"Look," she said, "I—"

He held up a three-fingered hand. "Please," he insisted gently, "I will not be long, I promise."

The lieutenant regarded her visitor. He seemed to mean it. "All right," she told him, folding her arms across her chest.

Cobaryn offered her another smile—his best one yet. "First," he said, "I would like to apologize for my behavior back at Earth Base Fourteen. In retrospect, I see that my attentions must have been a burden to you. In my defense, I can only state my ignorance of human courtship rituals."

An apology was the last thing she had expected. "Don't worry about it," she found herself saying. "In a way, it was kind of flattering."

The captain inclined his hairless head. "Thank you for understanding. There is only one other thing. . . ."

But he didn't say what it was. At least, not right away. Whatever it was, he seemed nervous about it.

As much as he had annoyed her at the base, Kelly couldn't help sympathizing with the man. "One other thing?" she echoed, trying to be helpful.

"Yes," said Cobaryn. He seemed to steel himself. "If it is not too much trouble, I would like a favor from you."

She looked at him askance, uncertain of what he was asking but already not liking the sound of it. "What kind of favor?"

His eyes seemed to soften. "The kind a knight of old received from his lady fair, so he could carry it with him on his journeys and accomplish great things in her name."

Kelly felt her heart melt in her chest. It was far and away the most romantic thing anyone had ever suggested to her, and it caught her completely off guard. For a second or two, she couldn't speak.

Cobaryn winced. "You do not think it is a good idea?"

The lieutenant shook her head, trying to regain her composure. "I . . . I'm not sure what I think."

He shrugged. "Again, I must apologize. It seemed like a good solution to both our problems. After all, if I had a favor, I could perhaps feel content worshiping you from afar."

Kelly sighed. She hadn't intended to. It just came out.

This is crazy, she told herself. Cobaryn was an alien—a being from another world. What did he know of knightly virtues? Or of chivalry? And yet she had to admit, he embodied them better than any human she had ever met.

"I . . . see you've been doing some reading," she observed.

"A little," Cobaryn admitted. He looked sad in a peculiarly Rigelian way. "Well, then, good luck, Lieutenant Kelly. I trust you and I will meet again someday."

He extended his hand to shake hers. For a moment, she considered it. Then, certain that she had gone insane, she held up her forefinger.

"Give me a second," she said.

There was a set of drawers built into the bulkhead beside her bed. The lieutenant pulled open the third one from the top and rifled through it, searching for something. It took a while, but she found it.

Then she turned around and tossed it to Cobaryn. He snatched it out of the air, opened his hand, and studied it. Then he looked up at Kelly, a grin spreading awkwardly across his face.

"Thank you," he told her, with feeling.

She smiled back, unable to help herself. "Don't mention it."

Still grinning, the captain tucked her favor into an inside pocket of his uniform, where it created only a slightly noticeable bulge. Then, with obvious reluctance, he turned, opened the doors to her quarters, and left her standing there.

As the doors whispered closed again, Kelly had to remind herself to breathe. *Come on,* she thought. *Get a grip on yourself.*

Cobaryn's gesture was a romantic notion, no question. But it hadn't come from Prince Charming. It had come from a guy she didn't have the slightest feelings for.

A guy from another planet, for heaven's sakes.

Now, the lieutenant told herself, if it had been the Cochrane jockey who had asked for her favor . . . *that* would have been a different story. That would have been unbelievable.

Chuckling to herself, she pulled down on the front of her uniform and put on her game face. Then she tapped the door controls, left her quarters, and reported to the bridge.

Where she would, in her own unobtrusive way, give Captain Shumar the dirtiest look she could muster.

Hiro Matsura got up from his center seat on the *Yellowjacket* and faced his viewscreen, where the image of Director Abute had just appeared.

The captain wasn't required to get up. Certainly, none of his bridge officers had risen from their consoles. But Matsura wanted to show his appreciation of the moment, his respect for its place in history.

For weeks they had talked about a Starfleet. They had selected captains and crews for a Starfleet. And now, for the first time, there would actually *be* a Starfleet.

"I bid you a good morning," said Abute, his dark eyes twinkling over his aquiline nose. "Of course, for the United Federation of Planets it is *already* a good morning. More than two hundred of our bravest men and women, individuals representing fourteen species in all, are embarking from Earth orbit to pursue their destinies among the stars.

"Before long," the director told them, "there will be many more of you, plying the void in the kind of ships we've only been able to dream about. But for now, there is only you—a handful of determined trailblazers who will set the standard for all who follow. The Federation is watching each and every one of you, wishing you the best of good fortune. Make us proud. Show us what serving in Starfleet is all about."

And what *was* it about? the captain wondered. Unfortunately, it was still too soon to say.

Of course, Matsura knew what he wanted it to be. The same thing Admiral Walker wanted it to be—a defense force like no other. But as long as Clarisse Dumont's camp had a say in things, that future was uncertain.

Abute smiled with undisguised pride. "You have my permission to leave orbit," he told them. "Bon voyage." A moment later his image vanished, and their orbital view of Earth was restored.

Matsura didn't take his eyes off the viewscreen. He wanted to remember how the sunlight had hit the cloud-swaddled Earth when he left on his first Starfleet mission. He wanted to tell his grandchildren about it.

"Mr. Barker," he said finally, "bring us about."

There was no response.

The captain turned to his left to look at his helmsman. The blond man ensconced behind the console there was staring back at him, looking a little discomfited. And for good reason.

His name wasn't Barker. It was McCallum. Barker had piloted Matsura's ship when it flew under the aegis of Earth Command.

The captain had wanted to take the helmsman with him when his ship became Starfleet property. However, he had been forced to adhere to Abute's quotas, and that meant making some hard decisions.

"Mr. *McCallum*," he amended, "bring us about."

"Aye, sir," said the helmsman.

The view on the screen gradually slid sideways, taking the clouds and the sunlight and a blue sweep of ocean with it. In a matter of moments, Earth had slipped away completely and Matsura found himself gazing at a galaxy full of distant suns.

They had never seemed so inviting. "Full impulse," he told McCallum.

"Full impulse," the man confirmed.

The stars seemed to leap forward, though it was really their Christopher 2000 that had forged ahead. As it plunged through the void, reaching for the limits of Earth's solar system and beyond, Matsura lowered himself into his captain's chair.

McCallum, he told himself, resolving not to forget a second time. *Not Barker. McCallum.*

Aaron Stiles eyed the collection of haphazardly shaped rocks pictured on his viewscreen, some of them as small as a kilometer in diameter and some many times that size. A muscle twitched in his jaw.

"Mr. Weeks," he said, glancing at his weapons officer, "target the nearest of the asteroids and stand by lasers."

"Aye, sir," came the reply.

Out of the corner of his eye, the captain could see Darigghi crossing the bridge to join him. "Sir?" said the Osadjani.

Stiles turned to look up at him. "Yes, Commander?"

Darigghi tilted his long, hairless head, his deepset black eyes fixed intently on the captain's. "Sir, did I hear you give an order to target one of the asteroids?"

Stiles nodded. "You did indeed, Commander." Then he turned back to Weeks. "Fire lasers, Lieutenant."

The weapons officer tapped a control stud. On the viewscreen, a red-tinged chunk of rock was speared mercilessly by a pair of blue energy beams. Before long it had been transformed into space dust.

Stiles heard the Osadjani suck in a breath. "Sir," he said, "are you certain you wish to do this?"

The captain shrugged. "Why wouldn't I?"

Darigghi licked his fleshy lips. "This asteroid belt is a most intriguing phenomenon," he replied. "I believe that is why we were asked to analyze it in the first place."

"And analyze it we did," Stiles pointed out. Then he glanced at Weeks again. "Target another one, Lieutenant."

The weapons officer bent to his task. "Aye, sir."

The first officer licked his lips a second time. "But, sir, it is irresponsible of us to destroy what natural forces created."

The captain eyed Darigghi. "Irresponsible, you say?"

The Osadjani nodded. "Yes, sir."

Stiles grunted. "I suppose that would be one way to look at it. But let me offer you another one, Commander. You see, during the war, the Romulans used this asteroid belt to hide their warships. When we finally found them and dug them out, it cost us the lives of three good captains and their crews."

Darigghi's eyes narrowed. "But what—?"

"What does that have to do with the activity at hand?" Stiles said, finishing his exec's question for him. "Simple, Commander. No hostile force is ever going to hide in this belt again."

The alien didn't know what to say to that. Of course, that was exactly the result the captain had desired.

Turning to the viewscreen, Stiles settled back in his seat. Then he said, "Fire, Mr. Weeks."

The weapons officer fired. As before, their lasers ate away at a sizable hunk of rock, reducing it to debris in no time.

Darigghi looked on helplessly, licking his lips like crazy. Ignoring him, Stiles ordered Weeks to target another asteroid.

Alonis Cobaryn sat at a long rough-hewn table in the gargantuan Hall of the Axe, which was located on a world called Middira.

By the light of the modest braziers that lined the soaring black walls, Cobaryn could make out the immense crossed set of axes wielded in battle by the founder of Middiron civilization—or so the legend went. He could also make out the pale, hulking forms of his hosts and the mess of monstrous insect parts they considered a delicacy.

First Axe Zhrakkas, the largest and most prominent member of the Middiron Circle of Axes, offered the captain a brittle, amber-colored haunch. "Eat," he said insistently.

Truthfully, Cobaryn had no desire to consume the haunch. However, his orders called for him to embrace local customs, so he took it from the First Axe and sank his teeth into it.

He found that it was completely tasteless—at least to his Rigelian senses. Considering this a blessing, he ripped off a piece of the haunch with his teeth and began chewing it as best he could.

"Have you reviewed our proposal?" the captain asked Zhrakkas, speaking with his mouth full in the manner of his dining companions.

The First Axe's slitted blue eyes slid in his guest's direction. "I have," he growled, spitting insect splinters as he spoke.

"And what is your reaction?" Cobaryn demanded. After all, he had been told to be firm with the Middirona—firm and blunt.

"I did not see anything that made my blood run hot," said the First Axe. "There is that, at least."

The Rigelian took another bite of the insect haunch. "Then you understand we mean you no harm? That the creation of our Federation does not portend badly for you?"

Zhrakkas grunted. "I understand that you say it."

"I do more than say it," Cobaryn assured him, forcing a note of titanium into his voice. "I mean it."

The First Axe made a face. "We will see."

It was the best response the Rigelian could have hoped for. Pressing the matter might only have made his host wary, so he let it drop. Besides, there was another subject he wished to pursue.

"I want to ask you something," said Cobaryn.

Zhrakkas shrugged his massive, blue-veined shoulders. "Ask."

The captain leaned forward. "As I understand it," he said, "you trade regularly with the Anjyyla."

The First Axe lifted his protruding chin. "Among others."

"However," Cobaryn noted, "the area between here and Anjyyl is reputed to be rife with interstellar strings, which, as you know, would be most dangerous to a vessel passing near them. I was wondering—"

Zhrakkas's eyes grew dangerous under his brow ridge. "The space between here and Anjyyl is *ours*—no one else's. If your Federation has any intention of trespassing in Middiron territory—"

The captain hadn't expected such a violent reaction—though perhaps he should have. "You misunderstand, First Axe. We have no intention of trespassing. We merely seek to increase our store of knowledge."

The Middirona's mouth twisted with mistrust. "Why would you need to increase your knowledge of what takes place in *our* space?"

By then, Zhrakkas's fellow councilors had taken an interest in the conversation as well. They glared at their guest with fierce blue eyes, awaiting his response.

The Rigelian sighed. Obviously, he had placed his mission here in some jeopardy. He would have to salvage it somehow—and quickly—or be the cause of a potentially bloody conflict.

Unfortunately he could think of only one way to do that. Gritting his teeth, he pulled his fist back and drove it into Zhrakkas' shoulder with all the power he could muster.

Though he was clearly unprepared for the blow, the Middirona barely budged. Then he looked to Cobaryn for an explanation.

"The First Axe needs to hone his sense of humor," said the captain, effecting his best human grin.

Befuddled, Zhrakkas looked at him. "My sense of humor?"

"Absolutely," Cobaryn pressed. "I thought when I poked my haft where it did not belong, you would find my impertinence amusing. But, no—you took my question seriously. Admit it."

The First Axe looked around the table at his peers. "I did no such thing. I knew it was a joke all along." He smiled, exposing his long, hollow fangs. "But I decided to turn the tables and play a joke on *you.*"

And then Zhrakkas expressed his feeling of good fellowship the way any Middirona would have—by hauling his meaty fist back and returning the captain's blow with twice the force.

Cobaryn saw it coming, but dared not try to get out of the way. Not if he wanted to hang onto the respect of the Middirona.

The First Axe turned out to be even stronger than he looked. His punch knocked the Rigelian backwards head over heels. The next thing he knew, Cobaryn was sprawled on the floor—and his shoulder hurt too much for him to even contemplate moving it.

Seeing him lying there, Zhrakkas got up and walked over to him. Then he pulled the captain to his feet.

"I like you," the Middirona said. "Your people and mine will be two blades of the same axe."

Trying not to wince at the pain in his shoulder, Cobaryn nodded. "I certainly hope so."

Connor Dane leaned back in his chair and studied the stars on the screen in front of him. They didn't look much different from any other stars he had seen, even if they constituted the part of space now known as the Romulan Neutral Zone.

Dane's eyes narrowed. "Let me get this straight."

"All right," said his science officer, a white-haired man named Hudlin. He was standing next to the captain with his arms folded across his chest, an expression of impatience on his wrinkled face.

"Our long-range scanners," Dane began, "have detected a wormhole out there in the Neutral Zone. And like any other wormhole, it's probably not going to be there for long."

"That's correct," Hudlin confirmed.

"But while it *is* there," said the captain, "you'd like the chance to study it at close range—even if it means entering the Neutral Zone, violating the treaty we just signed, and risking another war."

The science officer frowned. "With all due respect, sir, we don't have to go very far into the Neutral Zone, and it's highly unlikely that the Romulans would notice us. As you're no doubt aware, the war served to thin out their fleet considerably."

True, Dane conceded. Of course, the same could be said of the Federation. "So you really don't think we'd get caught?"

"I really don't," said Hudlin.

The captain grunted. "I'll tell you what, pal—I think you're in luck. You see, between you and me and the bulkhead, I don't give a rat's fat patootie about this Romulan Neutral Zone everybody's so impressed with. On the other hand, I don't give a rat's fat patootie about your wormhole."

The science officer stared at him, clearly more than a little confused. "But you said I was in luck."

"You are. You want to get a little closer to that wormhole? Be my guest. Just don't get me involved, all right? I hate the idea of having to explain something like this to a court-martial."

And with that, Dane got up from his chair and headed for the turbolift. Naturally, he didn't get far before he heard from Hudlin again.

"Sir?" said the science officer, hurrying to catch up with his captain. He looked around at the other bridge personnel, who were looking on with undisguised curiosity. "Where are you going?" he asked.

Dane shrugged. "To my quarters. I figure I'll get a little shuteye. But don't worry—you've got all the leeway you need. Just try to bring the ship back in one piece, okay?"

Again he headed for the turbolift.

"No!" Hudlin exclaimed.

The captain looked back at him. "No?"

The science officer swallowed. "What I mean is . . . I can't command the ship. I'm only a science officer."

Dane feigned surprise. "Hang on a second, Mr. Hudlin. There's a wormhole out there just begging to be examined with short-range sensors—and you're going to let that kind of opportunity slip through your fingers? What kind of scientist are you?"

The man couldn't have looked more frustrated. "But I've had no tactical training. What if—"

The captain regarded him. "What if you run into some Romulans?" He allowed a note of irony to creep into his voice. "It's highly unlikely that they'd notice us, don't you think? Especially after the war thinned out their fleet so much."

The other man frowned. "There's no need to be abusive," he responded. And without another word, he retreated to his science station.

Dane returned to his center seat, where he was greeted again by the stars that filled the Neutral Zone. "There's no need to be abusive, *sir*," he said under his breath.

* * *

Bryce Shumar was three weeks out of Earth orbit when he finally found what he was looking for.

The Tellarite vessel on his viewscreen was a collection of dark, forbidding spheres, some bigger than others. The deep creases between them served as housings for the spacecraft's shield projectors, weapons ports, scanner arrays, and audio-visual transmitters, while a quartet of small cylinders, which spilled golden plasma from unlikely locations among the spheres, provided the ship with its propulsion capabilities.

More to the point, the vessel was far from any of the established trade routes. And from the time it had picked up Shumar's ship on its long-range scanners, it had done its best to elude pursuit.

Unfortunately for the Tellarite, there wasn't a starfaring vessel in the galaxy that could outrun a Christopher 2000. It hadn't ever been a question of whether Shumar's craft would catch up with its prey; the only question had been *when*.

Mullen, Shumar's first officer, came to stand beside the captain's chair. "Interesting ship," he noted.

"Ugly ship," Shumar told him. "Probably the ugliest I've ever seen. And when you run an Earth base, you see all kinds."

The younger man looked at him, no doubt uncertain as to how to react to the remark. "I have to admit, sir, I'm no expert on esthetics."

"You don't have to be," said Shumar. "Some things are ugly by definition. That Tellarite is one of them."

"Weapons range," announced Wallace, the helm officer.

The captain leaned forward. "Raise deflector shields and route power to laser batteries."

Forward of his center seat, Morgan Kelly manipulated her tactical controls. "Aye, sir," came her reply.

Just like old times, thought Shumar. He turned to Klebanov, his navigator. "Hail the Tellarite, Lieutenant."

The woman went to work. A moment later, she looked up. "They're responding," she told the captain.

"On screen," he said.

Abruptly, the image of a porcine being with a bristling beard and a pronounced snout assaulted his viewscreen. "What is the meaning of this?" the Tellarite growled.

Shumar could tell the alien was covering something up. Tellarites weren't very good at duplicity.

"I'm Captain Shumar," he said, "of the starship *Peregrine.* I have reason to believe you're carrying stolen property."

"I'm Captain Broj of the trading ship *Prosperous,*" the Tellarite answered, "and what I carry is my own business."

"Not so," the human pointed out. "It's also the business of the United Federation of Planets."

Broj's already tiny eyes screwed up even tinier. "The United *What?*" he grunted, his tone less than respectful.

"The United Federation of Planets," Shumar repeated patiently. "An organization of which your homeworld is a charter member."

"Never heard of it," said the Tellarite.

Another lie, the human reflected. "Nonetheless," he insisted, "I need to search your vessel. If you haven't got anything to hide, you'll be on your way in no time. If—"

"Sir," said Kelly, a distinct note of urgency in her voice, "they're building up laser power."

Shumar wasn't the least bit surprised. "Target their weapons ports and fire, Lieutenant."

Out in space, the *Peregrine* buried her electric-blue fangs in the other ship's laser banks. But Shumar didn't see that. What he saw was the wide-eyed apprehension on Broj's face as he anticipated the impact of Shumar's assault and realized that the human had beaten him to the punch.

Suddenly, the Tellarite flung his arms out and lurched out of sight, revealing two other Tellarites on a dark, cramped bridge. A console behind them erupted in a shower of sparks, eliciting curses from Broj's crewmen and a series of urgent off-screen commands.

When Broj returned, his eyes were red-rimmed and his nostrils were flaring with anger. "How dare you fire on a Tellarite ship!" he snorted.

"As I indicated," said Shumar, "I'm acting under Federation authority. Now, are you going to cooperate . . . or do I have to take out your shield generators as well?"

Broj's mouth twisted with indignation. For a fraction of a second, he looked capable of anything. Then he seemed to settle down and consider his options—and come to the conclusion that he had none.

"All right," the Tellarite agreed with a snarl. He glanced at someone off-screen. "Lower the shields."

Shumar nodded approvingly. "That's better." He got to his feet. "Lieutenant Kelly, you're with me. Mr. Mullen, you've got the center seat. Keep our weapons trained on the Tellarite—just in case."

As Kelly slaved her weapons functions to the navigation console, the captain headed for the turbolift. To his surprise, his first officer insinuated himself in Shumar's path.

"Yes?" the captain asked, wondering what the man wanted.

"Begging your pardon, sir," said Mullen in a low, deferential voice, "but Earth Command regs called for commanding officers to remain on their ships. Generally, it was their subordinates who led the boarding parties."

"Subordinates like *you*, I suppose?"

The exec nodded. "That's correct, sir."

Shumar smiled at him. "This isn't Earth Command, Mr. Mullen. Starfleet has no regulations against captains leading boarding parties—at least, none that I'm aware of. Besides, I like to get my hands dirty."

By then, Kelly was ready to depart. Shumar clapped his exec on the shoulder and moved past him, then opened the lift doors with a tap on the bulkhead padd and went inside. After Kelly joined him, he closed the doors again and the compartment began to move.

The weapons officer glanced at him sideways. "So tell me," she said, "when was the last time you had occasion to use a laser pistol, Captain I-Like-to-Get-My-Hands-Dirty?"

Shumar patted the weapon on his hip. "Never, Lieutenant. That's why I brought you along."

Look for STAR TREK fiction from Pocket Books

Star Trek®: The Original Series

Star Trek: The Next Generation®

Star Trek® Books available in Trade Paperback

STAR TREK
THE EXPERIENCE
LAS VEGAS HILTON

Be a part of the most exciting deep space adventure in the galaxy as you beam aboard the U.S.S. Enterprise. Explore the evolution of Star Trek® from television to movies in the "History of the Future Museum," the planet's largest collection of authentic Star Trek memorabilia. Then, visit distant galaxies on the "Voyage Through Space." This 22-minute action packed adventure will capture your senses with the latest in motion simulator technology. After your mission, shop in the Deep Space Nine Promenade and enjoy 24th Century cuisine in Quark's Bar & Restaurant.

Save up to $30

Present this coupon at the STAR TREK: The Experience ticket office at the Las Vegas Hilton and save $6 off each attraction admission (limit 5).